The Rainbow
Through
The Rain

Other books by Hugh Cameron

The Technique of Total Hip Replacement
The Bone Implant Interface
Have Knife Will Travel
To Slip the Surly Bonds of Earth
    Book 1—*About the Breaking of the Day*
    Book 2—*Upon the Further Shore*

With Edna Quammie
    The Big House

Additionally, he has written several book chapters on technical subjects and more than two hundred research publications.

The Rainbow Through The Rain

Hugh Cameron
and Edna Quammie

Copyright © 2020 by Hugh Cameron and Edna Quammie.

Library of Congress Control Number: 2020902658
ISBN: Hardcover 978-1-7960-8723-9
Softcover 978-1-7960-8722-2
eBook 978-1-7960-8721-5

All rights reserved. No part of this book may be reproduced or transmitted in any form or by any means, electronic or mechanical, including photocopying, recording, or by any information storage and retrieval system, without permission in writing from the copyright owner.

This is a work of fiction. Names, characters, places and incidents either are the product of the author's imagination or are used fictitiously, and any resemblance to any actual persons, living or dead, events, or locales is entirely coincidental.

Any people depicted in stock imagery provided by Getty Images are models, and such images are being used for illustrative purposes only.
Certain stock imagery © Getty Images.

Print information available on the last page.

Rev. date: 02/07/2020

To order additional copies of this book, contact:
Xlibris
1-888-795-4274
www.Xlibris.com
Orders@Xlibris.com

Contents

Preface vii
Acknowledgments ix

Chapter 1	The Arrest	1
Chapter 2	Kandahar	5
Chapter 3	The Rape	15
Chapter 4	The Nursing Home	19
Chapter 5	Svengali	22
Chapter 6	Where Has Love Gone	29
Chapter 7	Charlotte Corday	35
Chapter 8	Le Diable Est Mort	40
Chapter 9	Oh, What Is Death?	48
Chapter 10	Dreams Die Hard	52
Chapter 11	Tomorrow and Tomorrow	59
Chapter 12	PTSD	64
Chapter 13	Götterdämmerung	67
Chapter 14	Happiness	72
Chapter 15	None Will Break Ranks	76
Chapter 16	John's Journey	82
Chapter 17	The Quest	92
Chapter 18	The Great Betrayal	95
Chapter 19	The Inquisition	101
Chapter 20	Oedipus Rex	105
Chapter 21	Out of Limbo Gate	113
Chapter 22	Nero's Fiddle	117
Chapter 23	Turmoil in the Old World	122
Chapter 24	High Noon	132
Chapter 25	Requiem	137

Envoi 139
About the Authors 141

Preface

Sheila was born in Toronto, into a cold, unemotional family where she was an unexpected and not entirely welcome afterthought. Seeking parental attention, she embarked on a self-destructive path. Eventually, after many missteps, she pulled herself together, emigrated to the US, got a student loan, and graduated as a nurse. To pay her student loans, she joined the US military. During her deployment to Afghanistan, she was exposed to unspeakable horrors. She fell in love with an army surgeon who had his own emotional problems. In spite of suffering from obvious post-traumatic stress disorder, she resisted being invalided home in order to remain with him.

Attempting to rescue a child being sexually abused, she accidentally killed a man. In consequence, she was given an other-than-honorable discharge (OTH) by the military. Suffering from PTSD and addiction problems, which she painfully overcame, she obtained work in a nursing home, where she fell under the spell of one of the residents who had a world-weary, cavalier view of life and who talked her into mercy killings, the first of which was to protect him from a demented, violent resident. She eventually reunited with her lover who had also been discharged from the military. They were beginning to settle down when, through a tangled series of events, she was arrested for the mercy killings and was jailed.

After she was freed from jail, they reunited and lived quietly and happily for a time before becoming involved in a violent denouement in a terrorist hostage situation.

At heart, this is a love story filled with all the dilemmas and uncertainties of death and the vicissitudes of life.

> I love thee with the breath smiles tears of all my life
> And if God choose I shall but love thee better after death.

Acknowledgments

In this book, there are extensive quotations especially from Rudyard Kipling. Also frequently quoted are William Shakespeare, Kit Marlowe, Robert Service, George Bernard Shaw, Lord Byron, Oscar Wilde, T. S. Eliot, G. K. Chesterton, Sir Henry Newbolt, Francis Thompson, Immanuel Kant, Schopenhauer, Nietzsche, Heidegger, Thomas Jefferson, Edward FitzGerald, the Brownings, Elizabeth and Robert, William Henley, Lord Tennyson, Ezra Pound, Wilfred Owen, John Donne, Ernest Dowson, Dylan Thomas, Adam Smith, the King James version of the Bible, Simon and Garfunkel, and numerous others. Any memorable phrase is probably a quotation, and efforts have been made to put all such in inverted commas. Intentionally, not all the quotations are entirely accurate as a few have been modified to fit the narrative. Special thanks to Monika Marks for her help and advice.

Chapter 1

The Arrest

There was a loud peremptory knock on her apartment door. Whether you have ever heard it before, in the Western world, everyone recognized that knock as the police. A loud voice said, "Police. Open this door, Ms. Lillehammer. We are here to talk to you."

Sheila's heart sank. That sense of guilt that lurked in every soul when so confronted rushed to the surface. She knew immediately what this was about. Her life was over. In panic, she thought of trying to run and hide. But where? She wearily got up and unlocked the door. *So this is what it comes to?* she thought. *It's the end of everything.*

It was her night off, and that evening, she had been sitting by herself in a darkened room, not knowing what had happened to John, her lover and roommate who had vanished the day before and whom she had been unable to contact. He had not shown up at his worksite and was not answering his phone.

As a former alcoholic, his sudden disappearance likely meant he had "gone out," as they say in AA—he had started drinking again. She was unutterably sad and weary. She had just finished listening on her phone to the YouTube video of that little girl Kaylee Rogers singing "Hallelujah" with the other little children. She loved that recording and that earnest little girl singing beautifully, especially the line "that rugged cross was my cross too."

How true, she thought as she picked up and then put down an unopened 40 oz bottle of vodka, which she had bought that afternoon in her despair.

Just because John is gone, she thought. *I must not use that as an excuse to start drinking again. Where did life go? It was not as if mine was that wonderful ever. What was it I read about Coleridge?* "With hope like a fiery column before thee, the dark pillar not yet named. Samuel Tayler Coleridge, logician, metaphysician, bard." *Same issue. His problem was cocaine. Mine are PTSD and booze. Oh Jesus, John is gone. Coleridge was right,* he knew.

> Alone alone, all, all alone
> Alone on a wide wide sea
> So lonely twas that God himself
> scarce seemed there to be.

Sheila thought back to the bitterness of her childhood—a father who seemed to love his four other older daughters but seemed to have little time for the youngest, an unintentional, somewhat unloved afterthought. A man who valued respectability above all, he thought of himself as a good man. He worked hard and brought in reasonable money to support the family. He had no great vices. He never struck his wife or children, but he was remote. At times, her shyness had rendered her inarticulate. She tried desperately to please him, again and again, but he never seemed to notice or care. When she made a mistake or sometimes even when she tried to help, he was harshly critical. Perhaps he thought she was not very bright.

The hurt was slowly replaced by anger that gradually built up in her. Because of his indifference to her, she began to think of ways to hurt him. She could not do it physically, but suppose one of his daughters turned out to be a bad girl? He would be mortified. That would get his attention. As she began to mature, her resentment progressively reached the stage when she was ready to do something, anything, to hurt or embarrass her father, and eventually, she thought she knew exactly how to do that.

She knew she was pretty. Her friends talked about who was fooling around with whom, but she did not know any boy well enough to ask one. The boyfriend of one of her much older sisters came to the house one day. The family was out for the afternoon, and she was on her own. Sheila opened the door and asked him in, telling him that her sister would be back soon. Her sister had told her that she had been drinking with the boy. They were both eighteen and, therefore in Canada, legally too young, but that had not stopped them. Sheila, thinking that that would make her seem more grown up, took a couple of her father's beers from the fridge and gave one to the boy. He popped it open and took a drink. She copied him and had a drink herself. It tasted foul, but she drank some more to show how grown up she was.

He had been staring at her chest. Her breasts had recently begun to develop, so she casually opened her blouse further to give him a better view. She leaned forward, and he cupped one of her breasts with his hand. "That feels nice," he said. He placed her hand on his crotch. She felt the erection. He squeezed her hand around it and groaned in pleasure.

"When will your sister get back?"

"The whole family is gone for the afternoon. We are here alone," she said, fondling him. "We could have some fun."

"Where? Here?"

"My bedroom upstairs."

"Let's go."

He followed her up the stairs into her room. She turned to face him and sat on the bed. They both undressed hurriedly. She lay back with her legs spread, and he guided himself into her. She felt him enter, then she felt something else. He pushed harder. It hurt, and she groaned. He rammed himself into her. She felt pain, then something gave way, and he buried himself in her. He continued thrusting in and out of her. It hurt with every stroke, but she said nothing other than groaning, which seemed to excite him further. He suddenly pulled out of her, and she heard him gasp.

"Wow!" he said. "That was real good. We should do that again when your sister is not about."

He lay back beside her with his hands behind his head, but a few minutes later, he again began to stroke and squeeze her breasts. After some minutes, he became hard again and again entered her. This hurt, and she groaned with each stroke. As before, this seemed to excite him, and he plunged away for a long time before pulling out again.

"Jeez," he said. "Awesome, but I had better go before your family gets back." He dressed and left.

Well, that's done, she thought. That was the first of many. She wanted her father to know but was not sure how to make it obvious to him that his daughter was not a good little girl. She had no hesitation in giving herself to almost anyone who asked. She became very popular with boys. Then she missed her period. She did not know what had happened. It was another two weeks before she realized that she was pregnant.

She told her mother, who was horrified that a sixteen-year-old daughter of hers was pregnant. Her mother told her father who was even more horrified. They knew that that was happening in society and that abortions were now commonplace, but they were Roman Catholic, and abortion went against all her father's principles. But a sixteen-year-old daughter of his having a baby was even worse. He was furious with her and fell into despair. He ranted and raved and threatened to have the boy responsible jailed for statutory rape. She told him that there had been many men and she was not sure who the father was. He raged at her, calling her a whore and a slut. He could not understand how any daughter of his could turn out this way.

Well, she thought, *at least you now notice I exist. How do you like that? Maybe you now wish you had spent more time with me and been a little nicer. Have the baby, have an abortion—I don't care. It's your fault.*

She had the abortion. She was never sure how she felt about that. Later in life, she certainly had regrets; but at the time, it seemed the most reasonable thing to do. She did learn her lesson and from then on took birth control pills. A few months later, she had pain and discharge. She was still too young to go to her doctor on her own, so her mother took her to her family doctor. Tests showed she had gonorrhea. Her mother was mortified. Her father was so angry he threatened to kick her out of the house.

His anger and disgust with her fueled her rebellion that continued until eventually, fed up with being lectured, she dropped out of school, left home, and after being on the streets for some time, joined a commune where she and others were proponents of free love. Finally realizing the futility of that life, she went to the States, became a nurse, and subsequently joined the US military.

That tortuous road had led to Afghanistan. There, she thought she had found happiness with John, a military surgeon who also had his problems. A terrible mistake in Afghanistan led to her discharge from the military, then to a period of aimless addiction to drugs and alcohol. Eventually she managed to pull herself up and recover from that, and she and the surgeon were reunited and were settling down, but suddenly he had disappeared. And now this knock at the door meant that she was looking at imprisonment, possibly for life, because she had done a few mercy killings in the old age home where she was working. The despair almost overwhelmed her.

Chapter 2

Kandahar

They were in a convoy a long way from Kandahar. Sheila was in a crowded Humvee made more crowded because the soldiers had placed some homemade plate amour along the walls. The manufacturers had not yet gotten around to armouring these vehicles against roadside attacks or improvised explosive devices (IEDs).

It was always the same—the heat, the dust, and the ever-present fear of IEDs. Several of her friends had died in this useless country. She had heard a commentator describing this place. He had said that the US had been there for seven years and nothing had changed. All these young American men and women dying for what? Democracy in this shithole? The commentator had said that when they eventually went home, it would be as if they had never been there. *What an utter waste of time,* she thought.

A roadside bomb went off. The Humvee ahead was thrown in the air, disappearing in the blast. Her own was also thrown up and landed on its side. The occupants were tossed around. Unlike most attacks, which were usually simply isolated bombs, there was an accompanying ambush. They could hear gunfire. The soldiers pushed the door open and climbed out. The last soldier out reached in and pulled Sheila and the other nurse clear. She heard the incoming fire going over her head and striking the vehicle. She dropped behind the truck, her hands up on her helmet to cover her ears. For a few minutes, there was the confusion of a firefight with the overpressure of the explosion, incoming and outgoing fire, dust, and men shouting. The firing died away as the last insurgent was eliminated or disappeared.

"Come on, Nurse," said the sergeant, "on your feet. There are wounded men here." The men were pulling the bodies out of the first Humvee. Most were dead. One had lost a leg, and a soldier was busy applying a tourniquet. Her training kicked in and overcame her fear, and she and the nurse who was with her rushed to help. Among the wounded, one soldier had a shredded arm and one had most of his face missing. Coolly and calmly, the two nurses and a medical corpsman got things under control—starting IVs, applying pressure dressings, and injecting morphine and antibiotics to ward off infection.

She was still working when she heard the medevac choppers coming in. The wounded were quickly loaded, and the helicopters took off for the base. The convoy reassembled and continued on its way. It was just another day at the office in this hellhole of a country.

Later, back at the base, Sheila searched for the soldiers she had treated at the ambush. By that time, all the seriously wounded had been stabilized and shipped out to the major military hospital in Landstuhl in Germany, where they would be treated before being sent back to the States for rehabilitation. This was her first deployment to Afghanistan, so it was all new to her. The next day, as things were blessedly quiet, one of the surgeons, whom everyone called Doc John, was going to give some help to the local doctors. He offered to take her and some of the other nurses to the community hospital where civilians were being looked after. The other nurses who had been in-country for some time shuddered and turned down his offer. Interested, she accepted his invitation.

Sheila had never been in a native hospital before. The doctor warned her it would not be up to Western standards, but nothing prepared her for the reality. It was utterly horrifying, like stepping back into the nightmare of the Dark Ages. There were rubbish and dirt everywhere. Patients lay on the floor or on a bare cot seldom with a mattress and no sheets. They were surrounded by shrouded figures covered from head to toe in a black bag with only a slit for their eyes. She touched one of their robes. *Polyester,* she thought, *in this heat.* There was no air-conditioning. The place stank. There was sepsis everywhere. The surgeon explained that there were some antibiotics—but only for the leaders or those politically connected—and very seldom anesthetics of any kind.

The Rainbow Through The Rain

One girl lay on a bed on her own with no one near her. She was horribly mutilated. Her face was simply one huge twisted scar with two sad eyes looking out of that ruined face.

"What in the name of God caused that?" Sheila asked the surgeon, bile rising in her throat.

"Acid attack. If they don't like what the girl is doing, they will throw acid on her face. Don't look so horrified," he said. "One of the British Army docs told me that they are doing the same thing in London, England. There were apparently more than one hundred acid attacks there last year."

"You're kidding. In London, England?"

"I wish I was. What I don't understand is that the eyes seem to survive in these ruined faces. I don't understand how."

"But the face. Isn't there anything which can be done for her?"

"Even in London, by the time they get some water on the face to dilute the acid or the poor kid to hospital, the acid has eaten most of her face away. I guess eventually face transplants may get good enough, but right now they are experimental. Only two or three have been done worldwide, so there is nothing that can be done, certainly not in this country."

"How can anyone do this to another person? Are the people who do this human?"

"I don't know. No one in these countries or even in London seems to think much about it. They tell me that British media hardly even mention it."

"Dear Lord! What are we doing in this country? After seeing this, I need a drink."

"So do I. Keep it to yourself, but I have got some vodka in my quarters. Come around later tonight, and we will have a drink and see if we can forget this horror show."

"Just tell me how to get to your quarters."

Later that night, Sheila found her way to John's quarters. He welcomed her, poured her a shot of vodka, and raised his glass to salute her

"You know, there is a poem which describes this situation we find ourselves in."

"A poem about this place?"

"Not specifically about this place but what is happening here.

> Things fall apart; the center cannot hold;
> Mere anarchy is loosed upon the world.

The best lack all conviction.
The worst are full of passionate intensity.
The darkness drops again,
And the rough beast, its hour comes at last
Slouches towards Bethlehem to be born."

"God," said Sheila, "the beast slouching toward Bethlehem, what an awful thought."

They shared vodka and talked. John was in a hurry, but Sheila uncharacteristically held back a little.

"Let me tell you another poem," said John. "This one is by Andrew Marvell written centuries ago.

Had we but world enough and time
This coyness Lady were no crime.
But at my back I always hear
Time's winged chariot hurrying near.
The graves a fine and private place,
But none I think do there embrace."

"Pretty convincing," said Sheila. "Just hold me and help me to forget what I saw today."

Their relationship quickly became one of comfort and companionship. He seemed to have an inexhaustible supply of vodka but refused to say how and from where he obtained it. To combat the problems of boredom when nothing happened, the urgency and stress in the operating room when the wounded came in, and the sheer terror when the camp was attacked with mortar bombs, they spent time together when they could. They were very careful and restricted their drinking to their time off. Neither wanted to put at risk any of the injured soldiers, who were their primary responsibility.

In spite of the horror and disgust Sheila had felt when she initially entered the native hospital in Kandahar; she was able to stiffen herself and continued to help when she could.

These are people, she would tell herself, *humans. Imagine being born into such an awful existence—trapped for life in a polyester bag in this heat with no education, no access to books, which most can't read anyway, unable to drive, unable to leave the house without a male relative being present.* She would shudder with revulsion. *To live that way from cradle to grave just like a battery* hen popping out one egg a year from menarche to menopause. With so many to choose from, no wonder it is not difficult to convince one or more of your children to be suicide bombers.

She had read somewhere that one woman in one of these countries had convinced three or four of her own children to blow themselves up as suicide bombers, and in recognition of her devotion to the cause, she had been elected to their government. She had heard that Saddam, when he was in power, would give $24,000 to families in exchange for a Shaheed, a suicide bomber. Sheila had no understanding of the thinking behind such behavior. Three dead children would maybe buy a house or at least an apartment. Doc John, who was very familiar with and clearly loved English literature, which, increasingly, he shared with her, quoted her a poem describing his view of the happenings, which he thought was a clash of civilizations.

> To wade through slaughter to a throne,
> And shut the gates of mercy on mankind.

At the civilian hospital in Kandahar, in spite of all their advanced Western medical knowledge, she was dispirited by how little effect she and Doc John were having. With almost no medicines and very seldom any anesthetics, there was in reality very little they could do. It was blindingly obvious that without Big Pharma, there was nothing. Back in civilization, people would complain about the major pharmaceutical companies—how they were providing unsafe drugs, charging too much money, and generally being bad guys.

The same people talked glowingly about so-called natural products. That had always amused Sheila. Surely people would realize that if any natural products were of any demonstrable value, the Big Pharma they were criticizing would have found it, patented it, synthesized it, and be selling it. She felt that these believers in the evils of Big Pharma should spend a day in a dump like this and walk a mile in these poor people's shoes.

The military warned both Sheila and Doc John to be careful outside the military camp as they would be targets. The Taliban did not want the invaders, the crusaders, the Feringhee, or whatever they were called, to be seen assisting the locals. Attempts would inevitably be made to assassinate them. John recognized the possibility but carried on anyway. One night when they had been drinking, he told Sheila his view of life.

And in a flash of flame I saw them and I knew them all.
And yet dauntless the slug horn to my lips I set and blew
Childe Roland to the Dark Tower came.

Sheila found it hard to believe that they would be targeted for trying to help until it actually happened. She and John were leaving the civilian hospital where they had spent the afternoon treating the sick and injured. Sheila was a pace behind. John was about to step out the front door. A man was standing just outside, glaring at him with fixed widespread eyes. He was bulky and wearing an overcoat.

Bulky, wearing a coat in this heat, and fixed glaring eyes—John reacted without thinking. He threw himself back inside the building, catching Sheila and hurling them both to the right inside the entrance along the inner wall as the shaheed, the suicide bomber, detonated himself. Being down on the ground behind the heavy walls of the hospital, the nails and other bomb fragments missed them. The overpressure from the explosion left them dazed.

They remained huddled against the inner wall. Sheila heard the screams of those wounded by the blast and began to get up shakily. John held her down.

"Stay down. There is sometimes a second one. Once the rescuers are clustered round the victims, he will detonate himself."

John did not let her move until ten minutes had passed and he was sure that there would be no follow-up suicide bomber. The carnage in the crowded hospital entrance was unspeakable. Most of the killed and injured were women and children. Their interpreter, who had not reacted quickly enough, was among the dead. Some blamed John and Sheila as they likely had been the target, and fists were shaken at them. That night, both got quietly drunk celebrating their narrow escape, their dance with death. What upset Sheila was the anger directed at them when they were only trying to help.

John laughed and quoted an old poem of the British Empire she had not heard before.

> When you're wounded and left on Afghanistan's plains
> And the women come out to cut up what remains
> Just roll to your rifle and blow out your brains
> And go to your God like a soldier.

They agreed that enough was enough. They had done what they could. They would not leave the camp again until their tour of duty was over unless commanded to do so. "'War without end,'" John said sadly. "'Let what is broken so remain.' Or if you like, 'This is no country for old men, sailing to Byzantium. The young in one another's arms.'"

Unfortunately, the pressure of events overcame that solemn promise. Things were quiet one morning, and Sheila was helping at the sick bay. A soldier ran in; he was shouting, "Nurses! We need nurses! We have info that there is a girl about to be stoned to death in a nearby village, and we have been given permission to stop it. Come now!"

Sheila had heard of the barbaric custom of stoning women to death, but she had never seen it happen. She grabbed an emergency medical bag, which was always kept handy, and ran out of the clinic to join the hastily assembling convoy. She jumped into a Humvee, and the convoy sped off.

"I hope we are not just being suckered into an ambush," grunted one of the soldiers sitting beside her.

"Who knows in this country," said the sergeant. "I don't know why we are bothering anyway. She will be dead long before we get there. It is that new lieutenant who thinks he can save the world. He needs to smarten up before he gets us all killed."

It was a high-speed run over terrible roads, and they were all shaken around inside the vehicle. Fortunately, in spite of their very real fears, there were no IEDs. Within half an hour, they topped the low hill and looked down on the target village. It looked like hundreds of others, hovels surrounded by walls in the middle of what looked like a stony, hilly desert. They could see a crowd in a dusty flat, open space on the outskirts. They were throwing stones at a cloth-covered mound sticking out of the ground. When the crowd saw the convoy roaring down on them, they scattered into the houses, leaving the place deserted.

Their vehicles rolled up beside the mound of shapeless rags that was mostly covered with stones.

"Ah Christ," the sergeant said. "These animals have killed her, but we had better look."

The men got out of the vehicles, and some started lackadaisically pulling the stones off the mound. Others stood guard, facing out, weapons at the ready, in case this was an ambush. There was a moan from under the pile of stones.

"Hurry, boys," said the sergeant. "She's still alive."

The men began to work feverishly. When the top of the mound was cleared, one used his KA-BAR knife to cut the cloth open. A battered, bloody face appeared.

"Nurse, help her."

Sheila pushed through the ring of soldiers working frantically to get the rocks off the victim. She held the girl's head as the men continued working to remove the stones. They found she was in a pit almost to her shoulders. As she held her, the girl's eyes opened, and she stared into Sheila's eyes for a long moment. Then her eyes closed, and she stopped breathing. The men tore at the ground, but she was buried too deep to allow them to attempt resuscitation. Sheila collapsed back on her heels, her hands, covered in the victim's blood, over her face. She sobbed, momentarily overcome by the surreal horror of it and her inability to help the victim. After a minute, she stopped sobbing and rose to find a wipe to clean her hands and sought out the local interpreter who had come with them.

"Why did they do this?"

"This one, I don't know. Usually it is because she was raped."

"She was raped, so she dies, not the rapist?"

"It is the custom. Occasionally, the man is stoned too, but when it is a man, he is placed in a pit at waist height. And if he can wriggle out when they start to stone him, he gets to live. A woman is buried up to midchest, so she can almost never get out."

"And we are here nation-building among these savages? Dear God!"

That night, as she lay in the arms of John, the surgeon, after some heavy drinking, she reached for the bottle. He stopped her.

"Christ, Sheila, don't drink it all. It's hard to get."

"If you saw what I saw today, you would drink it all."

"You mean the honor killing?"

"Is that what they call it? An honor killing?"

"Yes. The daughter got raped, so her father's honor was besmirched."

"So they don't kill the rapist. They kill the girl."

"Get used to it. Soon it will be as American as apple pie. Welcome to Minneapolis or Kansas or that place in Michigan. Young girls get their genitals cut off. If they are too Westernized, they get sent back to their shithole country to marry their first cousin, or they just kill them on the spot. There was that Canadian case where a man, his wife, and son killed his three daughters and his second wife who were living with them. Their crime was that the girls had posted pictures on Facebook in Western dresses. They hit them on the head, stuffed the four of them into a car, and drove it into a lake."

"In Canada? When? I did not know that."

"It was in the news. The son evaded the law and escaped back to Afghanistan."

"They do this in the States?"

"Apparently, so I hear, where there is a big enough group of them. Mainstream media almost never report it."

"What in the name of God is happening to our country?"

"Who knows? Our fearless leaders have been importing these people like crazy since the Twin Towers fell. It is almost like a reward. But I am told it is much, much worse in Europe. Ah, Sheila, there is nothing we can do. Don't think about it. Don't worry about it. In a million years, who will care anyway? Have another drink and forget about it."

"I can't stand the thought that the US will be like this place in a few years."

"Then learn to speak Japanese. They are among the few people who are content with their own society. Maybe Korea is too. I think that there was a big pushback recently against their government for taking in so-called refugees. The current leaders in the West seem to hate the West. This is not like the old days of the British Empire. There is a famous story told. I think it is about Napier when he was running India. The Brahmans told him about suttee, that it was their national custom to burn widows on their husband's funeral pyre. Napier told them it was a British custom to hang men who burned women. They could practice their custom if they wanted, then he would practice his. Suttee stopped pretty quickly after he hung the first few to show he was serious.

"Anyway, we are only small, unimportant cogs in the wheel. Do what I do. Read literature from a bygone era, drink a lot, and dream of the past, of 'old forgotten far-off things, and battles long ago.' Forget the ugly, depressing present. There is nothing we can do to change anything. We are Augustine of Hippo, and the Vandals are out there."

"I've never heard of him, but you are probably right. You must teach me some poetry so I can live in the past too. At my school, the teachers frowned on 'dead white men' like Shakespeare and all the rest. I've never read any of them. Maybe the past will help me forget the horror of the present we are living in. Right now, hold me so I don't have to think of these monsters in that village."

"Shakespeare, yes, *The Taming of the Shrew*. 'Ah, there's a wife, come kiss me, Kate!'"

Chapter 3

The Rape

Sheila felt she was teetering on the edge of a breakdown. She could hold it together in the operating room where it was all brisk purpose and efficiency, looking after these poor wounded, mutilated young men whose lives were destroyed by shaheeds (the suicide bombers), IEDs, and those traitors or murderers they had just finished training who turned their guns on the Americans who had just been teaching them. With IEDs, the blast was upward. What were blown off were legs and genitals?

As always, she did not understand what they were doing in that country and what, if any, the military objectives were. For what long-term goal exactly? She had no idea, and no one she knew did. The media and the politicians equally seemed to have no ideas, no overarching purpose, and no exit strategy.

She knew, like many of the other nursing staff, that she was suffering from some degree of PTSD (post-traumatic stress disorder). The feeling of fear, hopelessness, and worthlessness were proof. What drove her to get out of bed in the morning was the thought that she was helping her fellow Americans, ignored by a country that had forgotten them.

I could go back to the US. My deployment will be over someday, she thought. *But then what? What could be more meaningful than trying to save these poor young soldiers?* What had her life been anyway but a worthless hop into one bed to another or one bar to another?

When I have let myself be fucked by every man on earth, then what? She saw possible salvation in John, this heavy-drinking, depressed, incredibly literate army surgeon. He had quoted, while holding her in his arms, from his favorite poem *The Rubáiyát* of Omar Khayyam, which he had said was the only good thing ever to come out of Persia.

> A loaf of bread, a jug of wine
> A book of verse, and thou beside me
> Singing in the wilderness.
> The wilderness were paradise enough.

God, she had thought at that moment, *to be with him in a cabin up in the coastal area of Oregon or Washington. That might be a pretty good wilderness.* She had never been there but had seen pictures of that empty, heavily wooded coast with the giant waves rolling in from all the way across the Pacific. She thought with longing of the quiet green forest and the ocean—no injured soldiers and no Shaheed's and no IEDs.

There was another poem he had quoted that she could not remember from whom.

> For I shall have some peace there.
> For peace comes dropping slow,
> Dropping from the veil of the morning
> To where the cricket sings.
> Nine bean rows will I have there
> And a hive for the honey bee
> And live alone in the bee loud glade.

She thought sometimes, especially in the postcoital triste, that maybe she had found the man the merciful God had finally sent to her. At other times, the dreadfulness of her current life—surrounded by malevolence, misery, and death—was almost too much. She had been brought up with a Roman Catholic faith, but as a child, that had meant nothing to her. She never believed a word about the man in the sky. The priests, her friends had joked, were only interested in little boys, so girls were safe with them. If her father believed in Roman Catholicism or anything else, she purposefully did not.

There were numerous military people around, but other than to John, she found it impossible to express her distress. Even with him, she tried to minimize her complaints in case he decided that she was clinically bad enough that she should be sent back to the US. Most of the other nurses were also having stress problems, and it was well-known that many had to be invalided out. In the lonely horror of Kandahar, she went to see the military padre. She was not sure why—"for confession, atonement, forgiveness?" She knew he probably could not help, but how could anything he said make things worse than they already were? The man tried to comfort her as best he could, for which she was grateful.

"I know it is difficult to believe in a merciful God in a place like this," the padre said. "I once read a description of this part of the world: 'the dark places of the earth, full of unimaginable cruelty, which have not changed since the days of Haroun al Raschid.' It disturbs my own faith. It looks as if God has forgotten or abandoned this place. But have you read Solzhenitsyn's *The Gulag Archipelago*? Even in the midst of the horrors of Marxist Russia, there were people of deep Christian faith, which gave them courage and dignity. Even in the worst of the gulags, the camps, a belief in God kept some of the people sane."

The sex, vodka, and the feeling of responsibility to her fellow soldiers were barely enough to keep her going. She resisted being invalided out. John suggested she go, but she wanted to stay with him. And he wanted her with him, so against his better judgment, he let her stay. She thought she could cope. Then one night she snapped.

She was sitting with a group of nurses and soldiers, idly chatting outside as the air cooled down in the evening. She was very seldom outside as the mortar bombs would occasionally fall on the camp when night hid the terrorists. From the quarters of their Afghan troop allies, she heard a piercing scream that went on and on.

"My god, what is that?" she said.

"Oh, that's just these fucking bastards raping a little boy they caught earlier."

"A little boy is being raped, and you men are just sitting here?"

One of the soldiers shook his head in disgust. "It is the fucking custom in this fucking country. It is fucking mind-blowing, but the fuckers at the top have given us fucking orders not to interfere. It is a local custom."

"To rape little boys?"

"Don't be so surprised," said another. "Wait until you get rotated through the hospital in Germany. The same people it there too."

"Ah God! That child is screaming. Come on, you fellows, do something. Are you men, or are you wimps?"

"We can't, Sheila. We have been given specific orders from the top not to interfere."

Something gave way in her head. All the injustice, the terror, the brutality, the sheer evilness and horror with which she was surrounded and was supposed to be silent about, the aborted child, and the fear of old age and loneliness boiled over. "Fuck you. Fuck all you wimps. I am going to stop these fucking rapists."

She grabbed one of those fearsome KA-BAR fighting knives one of the men had been playing with and ran into the night. The men were stunned but, being soldiers, responded quickly and ran after her. She burst through the door into the very small room where the screams were coming from. It seemed crowded. Two men were holding a little boy while a third one was raping him. Surprised, the rapist pulled out of the boy and pivoted toward her. The weapon she was brandishing in her hand was a razor-sharp fighting knife. He ran right onto it. She watched in frozen horror as it entered his naked belly and went up under his rib cage into his heart, and he dropped to the floor

Stricken, she stood there. One of the other men let go of the child and grabbed her. The other one took the knife from her and, enraged, slashed her across the face. Immediately, her right eye went blind. The slash was from her hairline to her chin, across her eye and mouth. He was raising the knife to stab her when the soldiers burst in behind her. One of the soldiers, without any hesitation about the risk to himself, went smashing into the man with the upraised knife, driving him back against the wall. The man managed to stab the soldier before the others subdued him and his friend.

The sergeant surveyed the scene—one dead man on the floor, two prisoners, one of his own men knifed, a nurse with her face opened, pouring blood, and a naked little boy. *Kill these two bastards and we can hush it all up*, he thought. *But no, there would still be the child*. If he attempted to hush it up, news would inevitably get out, and he and his men would be crucified and go to jail. The nurse would have to stand trial. No matter how they spun it, the nurse was in real trouble.

"Sweet suffering Jesus Christ, what a mess! Get her to the hospital."

Chapter 4

The Nursing Home

"You have seen my nursing degree. I had a medical discharge from the US Army for PTSD, which I developed in Afghanistan like many of the other combat nurses. I was not well for a while, but I have had therapy and now feel quite able to work again."

"I see you worked in two nursing homes in the last year, both for less than six months."

"One was in Seattle. I had never been there, and to my surprise, I found that town filthy and full of drug addicts. I did not want to live there, so I quit."

"And Bozeman, Montana?"

"I found it nice but too small. I am from a big city."

"Yes, from Toronto originally, I see. So you are a Canadian?"

"A US citizen now."

"Of course, you were in the US military. I contacted the Seattle nursing home. They forwarded your records, which suggested that you had a problem with alcohol."

"That is true, but I have joined AA, and my dry date, since I last had a drink, is almost nine months ago."

"Really?" The administrator looked across her desk at Sheila for a very long moment, and then she sighed. "OK. We are short of RNs to administer medication to the patients and to supervise the ancillary staff. I will hire you provisionally. If in a month, things are going well, I will offer you a permanent position. You can start tonight. Let me orient you now and introduce you to some of the staff and residents."

Inwardly, Sheila breathed a sigh of relief. Her unenviable record of an other than honorable discharge from the US military made it difficult to even get an interview at any desirable hospital. Human resources at almost all hospitals knew that even those ex-military combat nurses with good records were finding it difficult to fit back into civilian life. Those who would have tried to help her in recognition of her military service were horrified when they saw her scarred face. The plastic surgeon had done his best, but he was an army surgeon, and she had never been able to afford one of the top-of-the-line cosmetic surgeons whom she was sure could significantly improve her appearance. The HR people used her discharge record to avoid being charged that they had refused to give her a job on the basis of her scarred face. She could not afford psychotherapy. She was not sure that would help her in any case. She knew what her problem was. She always had.

The only people who would take her were nursing homes or old age homes that are chronically short of RNs (registered nurses). She had lost the last two jobs because of alcohol. She had not fallen down drunk, but a family member had smelled alcohol on her breath. By traveling to the least desirable part of the US, the Rust Belt, she felt her job search might be easier. No one who could get out wanted to live in this lousy climate, these dying towns with their escalating white death of drugs and alcohol and their disastrous inner cities. But she had done it. In Detroit, she had finally landed another job. Her funds were about to run out, so she had just avoided being homeless.

On her way back to the motel where she had checked in that morning, she stopped at a Mexican cafe and had a shrimp and chicken burrito and coffee. It had no taste at all, but it was cheap and filling and she had to survive until her first paycheck. She looked longingly through the window at the liquor store across the street. *One day at a time,* she thought, remembering the AA slogan. *Anyone can fight the battle for one day. I must find an AA meeting, but I start work at 7:00 p.m., too early for most meetings. I will have to find one held during the day.*

She got back inside her old car to drive back to her motel. It was in a poor area but was cheap, which was all she could afford. *At least no one is going to steal a piece of junk like this,* she thought, looking at her car. *I'll start looking for a decent apartment tomorrow.*

Back at the motel, she turned on the TV, and then turned it off again. *God,* she thought, *all the news are bad news or probably fake, and all the shows, nonsense. Where has comedy gone? The only funny one is that one about the physicists,* The Big Bang Theory. *Well, at least I have my books. Doc John taught me many things, including a love of the literature of times gone by and, unfortunately, a love of vodka. As he would say, "There is not an emotion you can have that someone has not written a great poem about—other men's words to describe you own soul." He was right,*

>but when so sad thou canst not sadder cry
>And upon thy so sore loss

I wonder where he is now. God, I miss him so much. I hope he managed to get into AA and is not lying face down in the gutter somewhere. If I can hang on to this job, I must try to find him.

The sudden depression swept over her. Tears filled her eyes, and she sobbed. Through her tears, she thought, *Maybe he and I could ride this thing out together. Ah God, where did it all go?* Eli Eli. Lemma sabachthani, *My God, my God why have you forsaken me?* She sat up. *Pull yourself together, woman. You did it to yourself. You and that bastard of a father of yours. Ah God, maybe it was not him at all; maybe it was just me.*

She showered and dressed in her nurse's uniform, applied makeup to try to at least partly conceal the scar on her face, and went off to the nursing home for her first night shift.

Chapter 5

Svengali

Sheila made rounds with the medication cart, giving medications to the residents who required it. She had to give the injections, mostly insulin to the unstable diabetics who could not manage on their own, and whose blood sugar she checked prior to giving them the insulin. Some of the residents to whom she had to give medication were quiet and apathetic. *Waiting patiently for the gates of death to open*, she thought.

There was, of course, as always, a couple of aggressive ones suffering from advanced Alzheimer's. The worst of these would make the lives of the other inhabitants of the nursing home pure hell with their threatening and sometimes violent behavior. If it was a particularly bad episode, they would have to ask the doctor who consulted at the nursing home for written permission to restrain them. That was such a headache, so they seldom did it. It was no longer legal to restrain these people indefinitely or lock them in their rooms. Sometimes, if the disturbance was bad enough, they were supposed to call the police, but they almost never came. The police did not want to be involved in what was for them a no-win situation.

The last resident she came to was in a corner room by himself. She glanced out of the window. It was still light enough to see that it overlooked the garden at the back of the nursing home. He was a little old man wrapped in a silk dressing gown of all things, sitting in a recliner beside his bed. She gave him his cardiac medications.

"Here, Mr. Saint-Exupery, your meds."

"You forgot the *de*, but bonsoir, pretty lady," he said. "My name is Maximilian de Saint-Exupery. But you can call me Max."

"Why, thank you, kind sir," she said, smiling, gesturing to the scar on her face. "No one has called me pretty in a very long time."

"Pff!" he said. "A bagatelle, a life lived. Where did you get that?"

"Serving in the army in Afghanistan."

"Then you have 'drunk delight of battle with your peers far on the ringing plains of windy Troy'—a bemedaled hero, a Joan of Arc, the Maid of Orleans."

"No. I killed one of the men who gave me that," she said, pointing to her scar. "But he was a so-called ally, so they gave me an other than-honorable discharge."

"Ah, but you must tell no one of that. It will be our little secret. *Pour moi*, for me, you are a hero who served your country. I have a little something to toast your triumph." He opened his bedside cabinet and pulled out a bottle of Armagnac and two glasses.

"No, sir. I can't."

He looked up at her with his head tilted at an angle and raised one eyebrow. "Can't?"

She lifted both hands, palms up, in the universal gesture of resignation. "Can't."

"Ahh, *mais oui*," he said sadly, "an unfortunate side effect of the war."

She felt a sudden shocking sense of relief that almost brought tears to her eyes. She immediately recognized that here was someone who knew her not-so-secret problem. Only occasionally at AA meetings had she had such a sense of relief. "You too?" she asked.

"*Peut Etre*, perhaps," he said with a shrug. "But I am eighty years old and don't care. A year here or there doesn't matter." Gesturing to the bottle, he said, "I would like to remember my youth. 'Come fill the cup and in the fire of spring'—

Sheila recognized that line immediately. John had often recited *The Rubáiyát* of Omar Khayyam. She chimed in.

> The winter garment of repentance fling,
> The bird of time has but a little way to fly

Max finished the stanza. "And lo the bird is on the wing."

"Amazing, a young American who knows poetry. How did that happen?"

"My boyfriend, John. He was a medic. He told me that poetry was what kept him going in the horror of Afghanistan. And he was right. I have clung to it since then."

"*Tres bien*, very good. And do you know any French poetry?"

"John said there was no such thing."

"Oh, he is cruel but not entirely wrong. Maybe *The Song of Roland*?"

"I have heard of the Chanson but never read it."

"Unfortunately, you have not missed much."

"I must finish my rounds, Mr. Saint-Exupery."

"Call me Max. When you have a moment, come and talk to me. We intellectuals are few and far between. We should have our own little tête-à-tête."

"Thank you. That would be interesting, Max. I will come when I can. Just don't let too many people see you with that bottle."

She settled in. The work was the same as it was in every retirement home in all the world. The residents who could move around independently and get to the dining room were not a problem. Inevitable violence from the couple of advanced Alzheimer's patients was always an unsolvable issue. Haldol, the drug for schizophrenia, calmed them down, but often, they did not want to take it. They would either refuse point-blank or take the pill in their mouth but spit it out when the nurse's back was turned. Sometimes, it had to be mixed with their food to get them to take it. The nursing home was very limited by law in its ability to use constraints.

There were always terrible stories in the media every few months of residents like these beating other defenseless residents to death. The courts did not seem to have any answers either when these perpetrators were charged with murder or manslaughter. These residents would wander around saying nothing usually, but their behavior was always threatening, glaring, and sometimes mumbling to themselves, which greatly disturbed the other residents. Sometimes, it was almost as if they had a fixation on one poor defenseless resident and would make that one's life a misery.

There was the endless changing of adult diapers and bed linens when patients were incontinent, the desperate frustration of just cleaning them up, and then the smell as they became incontinent again before one had even left the room. There were the unexpected slaps and punches from confused patients. There was the struggle of trying to turn the bedbound, optimally every two hours, to prevent bed sores from developing, an ultimately impossible job given the level of staffing.

Not that Sheila blamed the nursing home owner. No one could even remotely afford the one-on-one care that was really required. That was only possible in intensive care units in acute care hospitals at horrendous expense. She had heard that the Japanese were working on robots to nurse their own old people as human helpers were either too expensive or unavailable. In the end, that would likely be the only feasible answer, but at what cost, and who would pay for it? The relatives of the patients were already complaining about the cost of this nursing home, and while it was certainly a reasonable place, it was by no means a top-of-the-line establishment.

Sheila spent the first few nights getting everything into a smooth-running routine, or as smooth-running as a nursing home ever could be. Death, after all, was hovering in the wings, and a resident, or client, as the administrator preferred to call them, would die every week or so. They had an arrangement with a semiretired doctor to come and examine the body and issue a death certificate. If the family had not made prior arrangements, they would contact the funeral home they usually dealt with. Perhaps some money changed hands over that, but that was not Sheila's concern.

She had brief conversations with Max, whom she always saw at the end of her medication cart run. He told her he was a light sleeper and she could visit anytime. On the fourth night, everything thankfully was quiet for a time. The personal support workers (PSWs) usually were busy most of the night changing patients who had been incontinent or turning others to prevent the ever present threat of bed sores. That night, her most aggressive residents seemed to have taken their Haldol, or the Boston Strangler, as she had heard it being described when she had first seen it used on a psychotic patient when she was a student nurse, and, thankfully, were quiet.

It was after 11:00 p.m. when she had completed most of her paperwork and nursing duties. She tapped on the door of Max's room. He was dozing in his recliner beside the bed, a book on his lap. He was wearing his favorite silk dressing gown. Hearing her come in, his eyes opened.

"Bonsoir, good evening, pretty lady. Are you here for a chat?"

"All is quiet, M. de Saint-Exupery. I thought I recognized the name and googled it. Any relation?"

"Alas, I am not related to the famous author and flier. I think he was the first to fly through the cordillera Andes, and he crashed in the Sahara Desert and somehow walked out. Quite a man. But it would not matter if I were related. No one here would have heard of him."

"That is true, but it is not personal. No one has heard of any famous hero nowadays. Absolutely no history is taught. He would fall into the Western patriarchy category and therefore be completely ignored. I forget what he wrote."

"Several books—*The Little Prince*, which was quite good, and some books about flying, *Night Flight* and *Flight to Arras*."

"Worth reading?"

"Maybe, if you have time. A little dated, but plus ça change, plus *c'est même* chose. Nothing much really changes. Life is life."

"What is a Frenchman doing here in this nursing home in Detroit?"

"I came, I saw, I fell in love, several times, in fact. But my loves left me, took most of my money other than my little Ivy League pension. As Leslie Howard said in that old movie *The Petrified Forest*, 'I am the last of a dying race. I am an intellectual.' That means I taught meaningless but pretty theories of philosophy to generations of college students who neither understood nor cared."

"You are a bit harsh on them, are you not?"

"Most of them could not spell Nietzsche's name, let alone understand a word he said."

"Wasn't he the 'God is dead' fellow?"

"Yes, he did say that, but no one seems to know that he also said that 'we have killed him and it will take oceans of blood to wash away that guilt.'"

"What did he mean by that?"

"He foresaw the old religion would be replaced by the new religion of socialism and oceans of blood and the millions of corpses would result from the loss of Judeo-Christian beliefs and values. Incredibly prescient. Absolutely brilliant."

"Oceans of blood. God, how awful!"

"Exactly, but let us talk of lighter things, us, for example, or maybe *The Unbearable Lightness of Being*."

"That is a book, isn't it? I have never read it, so don't tease me with my ignorance. Why are you still here? Why didn't you go back to France?"

"I did, to Paris. But Paris is no longer Paris. Gene Kelly and Debbie Reynolds are no longer singing in the rain. They would be trudging through the sewage and the souks. I now have more in common with the US than with Europe. I have become an *Americaine*."

"Your family?"

"'Lo some we loved, the loveliest and the best' have gone on to another world. The ones who only used me, I no longer have contact with nor any desire for contact."

"So no lost love?"

"Gone with the wind,

Flung roses roses riotously with the throng.

Dancing to put thy pale lost lilies out of mind.

"My lost lilies, withered away a long time ago. But you, tell me about your family, your husband, children and friends."

"I guess I misplaced them along the way or forgot to have any."

"I am sorry, but you are young." He picked up a glass of brandy from the floor where he had hidden it under his bed, raised it to toast her, and took a long sip.

"'Ah with the grape my fading life provide'"

"You like *The Rubáiyát* so much I bought a copy for myself. As I read this afternoon,

>oh thou, who didst with pitfall and with gin
>Beset the road I was to wander in"

"Ah, *ma pauvre*, poor child," he said. "What can you do? What the hell can you do? That is true for all of us.

>The moving finger writes, and, having writ,
>Moves on: Not all thy piety nor wit
>Can lure it back to cancel half a line
>Not all thy tears wash out a word of it.

Perhaps we are a wounded pair, you and I."

"Oh, Max, if you only knew." And she started to cry.

"*Ma pauvre enfant*. 'Forlorn, the very word is like a bell to take me back from thee to my sole self.' I am sure love waits for you somewhere at the end of the rainbow."

She brushed away her tears. "Oh yes, did you ever read Francis Thompson?"

"'The Hound of Heaven?' Yes."
"That was—that is me.

> I tempted all his serviters, but to find
> My own betrayal in their constancy.
> I clung to the whistling mane of every wind
> But whether they swept, smoothly fleet,
> the long savannahs of the blue.
> Fear wist to evade as Love wist to pursue."

"Bravo, *cherie, magnifique*. I will have to reread my books to talk to you. Give me that one," he said, pointing to the end of a shelf of books. He leafed through it. "*Eh bien*, here it is, Francis Thompson.

> Across the margent of the world I fled
> And troubled the gold gateways of the stars.
> I said to dawn be sudden, to eve be soon.

That was me, us, once upon a time. But now, *pour moi*, for me.

> Yea, faileth now even the dream
> The dreamer, and the lute, the lutist.

Pardon, I am sorry to be an old man ruminating on his death.

> Where are the songs of spring?
> Aye, where are they?

But you are young, and the world is ahead of you."

"Yeah, sure!" said Sheila. "Look at me," she said, touching the scar on her face and her artificial eye. "My days of wine and roses are over. How would you say it, 'gone, gone, gone with Thebes the Golden.' But I must go on my rounds to check the residents. I will see you tomorrow."

"Ah, *demain*, until tomorrow. I look forward *avec Plaisir*." And he blew her a kiss with his fingertips as she left his room and quietly closed the door.

Chapter 6

Where Has Love Gone

"Merci, merci beaucoup," said Max as he gratefully accepted the bottle of Armagnac Sheila had brought for him at his request. She never asked how he had acquired it before she came to work in the home. He had told her the brand he preferred and had given her the money. He opened it, took a glass from his bedside cabinet, filled it, and toasted her.

"'Ah with the grape my fading life provides,' or something like that. How is your reading coming along? Have you read through that poetry book I gave you?"

"Yes. There are whole swaths of it I did not like at all. Other than a few verses, I mostly loathed Shelley, Keats, Rossetti, and the rest. What a bunch of soy boys, the original beta males. Were they really men?"

"In the gender sense? Yes, I believe they were. I think the gushing emotions over a flower or a Grecian urn was the fashion of the day. Ladies had vapors, and gentlemen had visions of unrequited love. It was the same in Europe, like Goethe's idiot young Werther, the suicide for love idolized in Germany, which is why so few European poems were ever translated into English. No one could be bothered. But they weren't all bad. Keats sometimes was quite good, like his alcoholic's song.

> Oh for a beaker of the warm South
> Full of the true, the blushful Hippocrene.
> That I might drink and leave the world unseen
> And with thee fade away into the forest green."

"But, Max, life and death, love and the pursuit of happiness, something that stirs the soul, 1 and they moan on bout Grecian urns and skylarks. There is nothing memorable about any of that stuff."

"Well, yes, I mostly agree, including that famous line, 'Beauty is truth, truth beauty.' Nice and I wish, but beauty sometimes conceals darkness, and truth is seldom beautiful. Plebeians like me feel that a poem has to be memorable. If the author can't or won't do the work to make it memorable, why should I waste my time with it?

"It is the same with modern art. Make an effort to communicate with me, jackass, or go away. Look at the difference between Picasso and Salvador Dalí. Picasso's masterpieces a child could do, two in one afternoon! Give me a break! Dali's *Christ of Saint John of the Cross*, on the other hand, is an unforgettable masterpiece. If I can't remember poetry, it is not memorable. The introduction of so-called free verse when they abandoned rhyme, especially iambic pentameter, was the beginning of the end of poetry. It was nothing but physical and intellectual laziness."

"So there are no new poems?"

"No, almost none that I would call poetry. Critics do, but I have been so disappointed I no longer even bother to look. As far as I am concerned, poetry died in WWI, that bloody cauldron that destroyed Western civilization. Those silly, stupid bellicose generals and politicians. Statesmen? Statesmen my ass! My ass is cleverer than these clowns. At least I can sit on it, which is more functional than these idiots. Oh yes, if the British had not become involved, Germany would have taken another slap at France, kicked some ass, taken some names, and then gone home. They did that after Sedan in 1870."

"I know nothing about history. We were not taught history when I was at school in Toronto other than about someone called Louis Riel and some sort of uprising in the Prairies in Canada. Why did they go to war?"

"I never heard of a Louis Riel and I do know most significant history. As to the origin of the Big War, who knows? The Kaiser was a bellicose moron, but if they had just ignored him, he would eventually have gone away and been replaced by his son. They went to war for Belgium. I mean, I like Stella Artois beer and Belgian chocolates and the Belgian food, especially their French fries, which are the best there is. But to start a war to defend French fries? For the neutrality of Belgium? I mean, who cares?"

"Was that why they went to war? I thought it was because some archduke got shot."

"That was the excuse—and a pretty pathetic excuse. If that was really true, then that Serbian gunman who shot Franz Joseph was right up there with the greatest killers in history—Marx, Mao, and Rachel Carson."

"Rachel Carson? I have never heard of her."

"She was the ecowarrior who made up the story or maybe believed that DDT was killing all the birds on the planet and got it banned. Before that, DDT had essentially wiped out malaria in the US and was well on the way to doing the same thing in Africa. These buffoons running the African countries still have it banned. Rachel Carson was the person responsible for killing more humans than anyone who ever lived. Millions of children still die every year in Africa because of her and her ban on DDT. They run around giving out mosquito nets rather than simply spraying with DDT. For sheer number of deaths, she makes Mao, Stalin, and Genghis Khan look like nice guys."

"Surely not."

"Surely yes. The world is desperate to be fooled. Look at the South Sea Bubble, the Tulip Mania, and all these Ponzi schemes of so-called unemployment insurance and old age pension. There never was any insurance and no pension funds, the politicians simply lie. They have always been Ponzi schemes. The unborn will have to pay, and the unborn do not vote."

"Max, Max, all of this is so depressing. Tell me something hopeful and joyous."

"You are right. Forget about it. Who cares? In a million years, it will not matter. Suppose I were young again. How about this poem?

> Out of the dark of the Gorgio camp,
> Out of the grime and grey,
> Morning waits at the end of the world
> Gypsy come away"

"That's better, Max. That sounds good."

"The heart of a man to the heart of a maid
Light of my tents be fleet.
Morning waits at the end of the world
And the world is at our feet"

"Bravo! 'Light of my tents,' how romantic. Last night I read Browning's poem. It was so beautiful."

"Which one? Oh, you mean Elizabeth's How Do I Love Thee?"
"Yes.

> I love thee with the love I seemed to lose
> With my lost saints - I love thee with the breath,
> Smiles, tears of all my life! - And, if God choose,
> I shall but love thee better after death."

"*Magnifique*! The best. There is nothing as good as that in the whole world. I just wish it were true sometimes."

"Oh, Max," she said, tears coming into her eyes, "I thought in Afghanistan I had come across someone who could love me like that. Then the disaster, and now I am all alone. And with this face," she said, touching her scar, "I will wander sadly down the empty streets of life, alone forever."

"Ah, *ma pauvre*. Life can be so hard and so unfair. *Mais* courage. Someday love will find you. But enough sorrow for one night. Read some more and we will talk again tomorrow. There is one poem you should remember.

> And not through eastern windows only
> When daylight comes, come in the light.
> In front the sun climbs slow how slowly
> But westward look and lo the land is bright."

Another late evening, her rounds finished and all temporarily quiet, she asked him, "Max, what is love?"

"Ah, *Cherie*, if I knew, I would have found it. Instead, in spite of all my brilliance as a youth, my studying, my knowledge, here I am, a lonely old man with none but your good self at my side. Love? Being a Frenchman, I thought I knew. What is Wilfred Owen's poem?

> I went hunting wide
> After the wildest beauty in the world,
> Which lies not in calm eyes, or braided hair,
> But mocks the steady running of the hour
> And if it grieves, grieves richlier than here.

"What do I know, *Cherie*? Thrice I entered the lists of love. Having lost twice, yet I was not afraid

> to hear with equal ear
> The clarions down the list.
> Yet set my lance above mischance
> And ride the barrier

"But again, sadly, I lost that bout also. Love left me, if indeed it ever even glanced my way. So here I am, 'out out brief candle. On the way to dusty death.'"

"You seem so morbid tonight, Max. Surely there is love somewhere?"

"Maybe when the young men, the knights, the troubadours lived only until their late twenties. The Black Prince was winning battles at age fifteen. Alexander the Great, king as a teenager, dead at thirty-three, wept because there were no worlds left to conquer. At thirty-three, maybe he was still in love with Barsine, and maybe she with him. But then again, maybe these were different men.

> I would not live in that man's company that fears his fellowship to die with us. We few, we happy few. We band of brothers.

"I thought when the world was young, my love was out there waiting for me and all I had to do was go and find her."

"When I was young, I was very promiscuous. I wanted to hurt my father, to make him ashamed of me. So I made sure he knew I was having sex with everyone. No love there. But when I found Dr. John, a drunk but a glorious drunk—he knew almost as much poetry as you do Max—I thought I had found love. They wanted to send me back home because of my PTSD, but I was afraid I would lose him. So I insisted on staying, and then in one night, in a few minutes, it all fell apart."

The tears came. "Oh, Max, it all fell apart, and my new life turned to shit." She wept.

Max waved his hands helplessly, wordlessly, unable to comfort her. What could he say? Then the thought came to him, the words from an old hymn, which he quoted quietly to her.

I trace the rainbow through the rain
And feel the promise is not vain
That morn shall tearless be.

She dried her tears. "Oh, Max. I am so lonely. I am afraid that I will be alone all my life." Then she straightened up and took a deep breath. "I have to get back to my rounds and see if the other staff needs help."

"Bonne nuit et bonne chance, chérie. A demain!"

"Good night, Max. Sleep well."

Chapter 7

Charlotte Corday

Sheila awoke from a horrific dream. As usual, all memory of it vanished as she sat bolt upright in bed, trembling with the unaccustomed noise of the telephone ringing. She had been asleep for a few hours following her night shift at the nursing home. As no one she knew was aware of the fact that she was in Detroit, she had no idea who would be calling. She answered the phone. It was the administrator at the home.

"Max has been attacked and is badly injured. He is asking for you. We have sent for an ambulance. Please come."

"Oh god," she said. "I am on my way."

She quickly dressed and was on her way out the door when the phone rang again. It was again the administrator. The ambulance had picked up Max, and he was on his way to the local hospital.

Max was still in the emergency department when she got there. She found him on a stretcher. His forearm was splinted, and his face was battered and swollen with what looked like facial fractures.

"Max. What happened?"

He could barely speak. It was difficult to make out what he was saying. His jaw was broken. "Crazy Bob attacked me. I am lucky to be alive."

Before she could say anything else, a porter came up.

"Sorry, miss, we need to take him to X-ray, and they have ordered a CT scan of his head. The doc says then possibly to the OR to get his arm and face fixed."

Knowing it would take time for these investigations to be done before any decision could be made, and then probably a trip to the operating room, Sheila went home, went back to bed, and tried to sleep. But sleep evaded her. She blamed herself. They all knew that Crazy Bob and equally crazy Jim were a potential danger and had threatened other residents, especially poor Maisie. But what could they do? There was effectively no mechanism in law to deal with these cases. After tossing and turning for an hour or so, she thought lying there was a waste of time, so she got up.

Not knowing what else to do, she walked around her apartment. *God, I would give anything for a drink,* she thought. But then she thought of the AA slogans 'Easy does it' and 'Let go and let God.' She fished out her twenty-four-hour AA medallion, the one they give to people who promise to stay sober for that day, and held it in her hand. "No!" she told herself. "Drinking will not help. It will only make matters worse. 'Anyone can fight the battle for one day.'"

She went back to the hospital. She found that Max had had surgery on his arm and face and they had planned to keep him in for a day or so to make sure there was no brain damage although the CT scan of his head had been negative. She made her way to his room. He was awake, and when she entered, his eyes lit up.

"Merci beaucoup, thank you for coming," he said with difficulty as his face was swollen and his jaws had been wired together to treat the fracture.

"Oh, Max, I am so sorry. How are you feeling?"

"Crazy Bob came into my room when I was sitting in my chair. He was carrying a cane like a club. I pressed the buzzer for help, but he attacked me without warning. I put my arm up to defend myself, but at eighty-five, Crazy Bob is still strong. I felt my arm break as he hit it with his cane. I was calling for help. He was beating me around the head when Jane, that little PSW, came in. She tackled him without a moment's hesitation. She was so brave. That young woman dragged him away from me. She saved my life. An orderly ran in, and they got him subdued and took him away, still struggling with them."

"My god, how awful."

"What was so awful were his eyes. I don't know if you have ever looked into the eyes of a wild animal—not a cat or a dog but something wild, feral. These eyes were terrible. I have previously always avoided looking directly at him, but I saw his eyes that night. There was evil there, the hate of a caged animal. No, even that is not right. I can't explain it. It was like looking into the eyes of a devil straight from hell. I have never seen anything like it before. It was terrifying. I will have nightmares about these awful staring eyes."

"Oh god, Max, I'm so sorry. I don't know what we will do with these two men in the nursing home. The staff, we have all been afraid of this. These two often terrify the other residents, especially Maisie, whose room is near the locked door through which in their confusion, they try to get out. We don't know how to stop it, or we do but we can't. We can't legally keep them doped up to where they can't move, and we can't keep them in restraints, except very temporarily."

A day later, Max was released and returned to the nursing home. He was slow to recover from the effects of his injuries. He had been mainly wheelchair-bound before, capable of walking only with difficulty to his en suite washroom. He had lost so much strength following the attack that it became difficult for him to get out of the chair and take a few steps. All Sheila's instincts were to help as she saw him struggle, but she restrained herself. She knew that such help was not help. He had to struggle to maintain his independence. Helping would be counterproductive, producing learned helplessness or treatment dependency.

In the months prior to the attack, Sheila had spent time with Max, usually in the early hours of the morning when the nursing home was quiet for a little while, or as quiet as it ever was with its ever-pressing need to change and turn residents, an endless "labor of Sisyphus" as Max called it. He told her that at his age, time was meaningless as he seldom slept through the night.

If he spent an hour or so talking to her in the night, then he could catch up with sleep during the day. He would, as he put it, "soon be sleeping forever," so "one moment in annihilation's waste, one moment of the well of life to taste." "Or better still to talk with you and remember 'old forgotten far-off things and battles long ago.'"

He also had prevailed on her to bring him his supply of Armagnac, which he would sip when he was with her. He no longer cared for the rich, smooth brandy beloved by the connoisseurs. He said his taste buds had shrunk as he had aged and what he wanted was something rough and raw. She said it was not good for him. He agreed but said it hardly mattered, and he did not care as he did not plan on living forever.

It was with literature and poetry that they spent their time. His erudition seemed endless. Her staff knew where she was and could contact her at a moment's notice. She was very meticulous and made rounds of the residence at least a couple of times per night, helping the PSWs with their numerous tasks. She would contact the relatives when it looked like a resident was nearing death or the doctor on call after the event.

Max had an endless store of both literature and poetry and would suggest which books she should read, which he would then discuss with her. His store of knowledge fascinated her.

"Are all Frenchmen so well educated?"

"Sadly no. Our education system is just as bad as yours. We do not teach the glories of the past. The young people today have never heard of Descartes and Blaise Pascal. Instead we teach the insufferable nonsense of these tricksters, these poseurs, Derrida and the awful Foucault, these so-called postmodernists. They are nothing but Marxists who, when their hideous doctrine was exposed for what it was by Solzhenitsyn, simply changed the names of the perceived problems from bourgeois to power and oppressed groups. Everyone is oppressed somehow by someone. They sold this concept to these naive, ill-informed people in humanities at the Ivy League schools, who proceeded to disseminate the poison to all American universities."

"That does not sound good. I did not know anything about this."

"It is not worth speaking about. It is so foolish, so we will not mention it again. In fact, most universities are now so corrupted one has to wonder if they serve any positive role at all. Think of the great Sorbonne in Paris. Some of its alumni are Uncle Ho, of whom the story is told that he ordered the arms cut of children immunized by the Americans. Maybe it is not true, maybe it is. Given the pathetic state of the news reports today, who knows? And yet, was it any better in the past?

"There was that American reporter who covered up Stalin's atrocities and was given a Pulitzer Prize for his lies. American college kids have never heard of him or Pol Pot, another noted product of our glorious French education, who starved or beat to death one-third of the total population of Cambodia. Not that you Anglos were much better.

"That awful London School of Economics has educated every African leader in their disastrous ultraleft wing policies, which universally led to nothing but starvation, except for maybe the worst of all, Mugabe. Your equally objectionable Fabian Society, who helped found that school for thugs, has the blood of millions on its hands. I forget the quotation—that 'it will take an ocean to wipe the blood clean from my hands.' Perhaps that was Lady Macbeth."

"Then how did you end up well educated?"

"I taught myself. Like your American, Harold Bloom"

"Tell me how you really feel about these postmodernists, Max. Don't hold back."

"*Pardonne moi*, Sheila. I am sorry. I should know better. An impotent old man vents his rage. I lost my battle against these poseurs. I think now every humanities department in every university in the US now teaches this insidious doctrine that will destroy the West. The death of the Enlightenment, tant pis, too bad. I will be dead before it happens, but those preaching this sedition will experience the full force of their unthinking treachery."

"God, Max, you sound like Kierkegaard, 'Life sucks and then you die." Tell me something pleasant."

"OK! You are correct, Sheila. Lighten up. Think nice thoughts. 'I chase the rainbow through the rain, and hope the promise is not vain, that morn shall tearless be.'"

"Good enough Max. Hold that thought. I will see you tomorrow."

Chapter 8

Le Diable Est Mort

Sheila saw Max on his first evening back from the hospital. The bruises on his face were still livid, and his arm was in a brace. With his jaws wired, he had to have his food pureed and fed through a straw. He had been very depressed, but on seeing her, he put on a brave face.

"*Eh bien*, Sheila, I have survived my appointment in Samarra."

"Evening, Max. Appointment in Samarra with, was it the angel of death? That was Chekov, wasn't it? No, it was Somerset Maugham who wrote that."

"*Tres bien*, very good. You should be a professor of English at an Ivy League school. You have read more widely than most of them."

"Oh, Max. I am so sorry."

"Tant pis. Whatever will be, will be, que será, será. My arm is not yet strong enough, so I would appreciate it if you would open this nice bottle of Armagnac you have brought for me. To drink brandy through a straw, what a comedown. What was it Shakespeare said about the seven ages of man? I forget where it was—'My big manly voice shrunk to a childish treble.' Yes, I remember.

> The soldier
> Full of strange oaths.
> Seeking the bubble reputation
> Even in the cannon's mouth."

"Like you, my noble warrior from Afghanistan."

"I don't think so. Nothing noble about that place. Trying to stay alive was all I wanted."

"Then tonight we should forget about bad things and read some Shakespeare, a sonnet.

> Shall I compare thee to a summer's day?
> Thou art more lovely and more temperate."

"Max, I think that was one guy writing to another guy."

"I think you are correct, but after a few hundred years, the Dark Lady, man, woman, who cares? Let me read some more sonnets to you. There are many of them, some of them quite good.

> When to the sessions of sweet silent thought
> I summon up remembrance of things past,
> I sigh the lack of many a thing I sought,
> And with old woes new wail my dear time's waste."

"Good, Max, but the girls are calling me. I have to go help. See you tomorrow."

The next evening, Max was somber. "I had terrible dreams. I saw the mad, feral eyes of Crazy Bob staring at me. It was horrifying. Can they not get rid of him? No other resident in this place is safe from him. He was threatening poor Maisie again today, I heard. She is terrified of both him and equally crazy and violent Jim."

"I asked the administrator. She says it is not possible. The police would not even charge him with assault because the DA says there is no hope of a conviction because he is mentally impaired. Even if they did, where are they going to put a demented eighty-three-year-old man? No jury will put him in prison, and if he is sent to a psych hospital, they will give him pills for a couple of days, say he is cured, and release him back to us.

"What is even worse is that he has a son who almost never visits but threatens the home with a lawsuit if we even think about keeping his father restrained, which we can only do for short periods if the doctor agrees. Sometimes it is awful. When he is really disturbed and violent, we have to wear football helmets, chest protectors, and Kevlar gauntlets in case he bites. They say call the police, but they take forever to come because they don't want involved in a no-win situation, and what are they going to do anyway?"

"So I live in fear. *Mon Dieu*, I wish I had enough money to ask you to take me from this place, but I don't. All I have is my university pension. My ex-wives took most of what I earned, and most did not want any children, and they certainly do not want to look after me. Not that I would want that either. Anyway, I could not impose on you. You have your own life to lead, your Wille zum Leben of Schopenhauer.

"Schopenhauer, I wish. Not much will and not much of a life, Max. I have my work, my AA meetings, and your company—my three pillars of wisdom."

"Ah, *Cherie*, this is no good. You must look for the man who was in your life, your Dr. John. Where and when did you last see him?"

"In San Antonio at Brooke Army Medical Center just before they discharged me from the hospital and the army. He was in a rough shape. They had tossed him out too. He still had his medical license, or I think he had. He was drunk when he came to see me, poor man. He tried." And she broke down in tears. "He was unkempt and reeking of booze. He said he was so sorry, that he should have had me shipped back Stateside long before my final breakdown. It was his fault, he said. He wanted me to be there with him in Afghanistan. He said that he was not worthy of me, that he was a failure, all his life he had been a failure and would never be anything but a failure.

"I asked him to stay, but he said he had brought nothing but misery into my life. He said again it was his fault. If he had me shipped back with a diagnosis of PTSD, the event would never have happened and that he would never forgive himself. I told him again it was not his fault and that I loved him. He wept and left, and I never saw him again."

"How sad. God, if there is a God, is certainly not a merciful one. That makes my current little fear a bagatelle, a nothing."

"We will try our very best to protect you, Max."

She helped him into bed and left him trying to get to sleep. She made her rounds of the corridors. All was quiet. She stopped in front of Crazy Bob's door. An unbidden thought came to her. *If I don't stop him, he will attack Max again, and Max is the only good thing I have had in my whole rotten life, The solution is not difficult.*

In confusion at having thought the unthinkable, she retreated to her office. Her mind was in turmoil. *I can't do this. Of course I can. I should not do this. Why not? Why should the one good man in my whole rotten life live in terror of this, what, this thing? Crazy Bob is not a man anymore. There is no humanity left, just a feral animal who will try to kill again.*

Head in her hands, she argued back and forth. Finally, in despair, she said "fuck it," went to the medicine cupboard, opened it, and loaded a syringe with insulin. Keeping it concealed, she made her rounds again.

All was temporarily quiet, and her coworkers were on their break, sitting in the kitchen. She went to Bob's room. The Haldol he had been given earlier when he was aggressive was still in effect, and he lay there snoring. She quickly found a vein and injected the full syringe of insulin. After withdrawing the needle, she kept some pressure on the venipuncture site for a minute so there would be no telltale bruising. She stepped out of the room and closed the door. No one had seen her. She disconnected the needle from the syringe and disposed of it in the sharps container and returned to her office. The other staff called her shortly for some assistance, and they were busy the rest of the night.

In the morning, the workers went to arouse the residents for breakfast. The PSW who entered Bob's room came to her with the news that he seemed dead. Sheila went back with her, carrying a stethoscope as she usually did in these cases. She listened to his heart and took his pulse and checked his pupils. There was no doubt. He had been dead for some time and was already getting cold. She went and phoned the nursing home's staff doctor to come and examine him and certify the fact and cause of death. She also phoned the administrator, who phoned Bob's son, letting him know of his father's demise.

"Oh well, it had to happen sometime. He was a sick man. Will you contact the undertaker?" was all the son said.

Sheila's heart was in her mouth until the doctor certified the death as being of natural causes, and she waited until the undertaker had come and taken the body away. She found it difficult to get to sleep that morning. When she came back to work in the evening, everyone seemed quietly happy. There was a palpable feeling of relief not only among the staff but also among the residents, especially Maisie that the threat of Crazy Bob was finally over. This cheered Sheila immediately, and a great load of guilt lifted off her shoulders. No one suspected anything other than natural causes.

Later that night, she knocked on Max's door and entered his room. He looked at her with raised eyebrows.

"Courage, *mon ami. Le diable est mort*," she said.

"Ah!" he said. "Your French is much improved. Some things we should never talk about in English in case walls have ears. *La belle dame* on the pale horse."

"The pale horse, the fourth horseman of the Apocalypse, really, Max?"

"*Peut etre*. There are some things we should only discuss in French. You need to learn a little more."

"Then teach me."

"With all my heart, my savior, my Joan of Arc. Now if *Le Bon Dieu*, the Good God, in his infinite mercy and wisdom would only take Crazy Jim to his bosom also, peace and tranquility would reign."

"It would be safer to say nothing. *Rien de rien*, eh?"

"Yes, but the human soul needs a confessional and sometimes atonement. It is difficult to take the problems of the whole world on a single person's shoulders. That is what the confessional was supposed to be. 'Oh Lamb of God, who taketh away the sin of the world, take away my sin also.' But the church has lost its faith. The last two popes were good, sound men, but this one, not so much—a liberation theologist, a Marxist in sheep's clothing. What is wrong with the Vatican that they could elect an Antichrist?"

"I never thought much about religion."

"Maybe we should talk about it a little, but it is so difficult, metaphysics. I do not know enough about quantum mechanics to even think about it realistically or even string theory, about there being other dimensions."

"I don't know what you are talking about."

"I am not sure I do either, but let us think a little. What is the Buddhist Nirvana or nothingness? God made the world out of chaos or the void, maybe dark matter."

"What is dark matter?"

"What fills space. I don't know, and the physicists don't seem to know either, but the universe is formed of it."

"What about the big bang theory?"

"Yes, but that just kicks the can down the road. Who or what created the ball before the bang? Ah, but this is too difficult. It is much easier just to accept something, some higher power. Faith is much easier and quite helpful.

> The depth and dreams of my desire
> The bitter paths wherein I stray

> Thou knowest who has made the fire
> Thou knowest who has made the clay.

"Tonight is a night to be thankful. Maybe we will think hard thoughts some other time. Here is another one worth thinking about.

> Far and forgot to me is clear
> Shadow and sunlight are the same.
> The vanished gods to me appear
> And one to me is fame and shame."

"Interesting. So I should have faith in something?"
"I think so. Why not?

> They reckon ill who leave me out.
> When me they fly I am the wings.
> I am the doubter and the doubt.
> I am the hymn the Brahmin sings.'
> Tonight we are young again, and I will live awhile.
> 'When all the world was young, lass
> And every goose a swan.

"I will have to look up the rest of that poem."

He took another long sip of brandy through the straw. "'Drink, drink, drink to eyes that are bright, as bright as the stars in the sky.' Sheila, I think I am drunk, but listen to an old man who is enormously grateful and wants your happiness. Look for your Dr. John. Miracles happen. He may be looking for you."

"Oh, Max, I can only dream."

"What is it? God, I can't stop talking tonight. 'I dreamed a dream of time gone by, when we were young, and love was'—my memory is not what it was. That was a musical, was it not? Search for him, Sheila."

Several weeks later, there was a difficult evening when Sheila, the PSWs, and the orderlies had to restrain Jim, who had been found in Maisie's room threatening her and one of the other elderly ladies with physical violence, something he had done before. They called the police, who, as usual, did not turn up. Wearing protective gear, they got him subdued, eventually got him to take some Haldol, got him into bed, and left him asleep. Exhausted and frustrated, Sheila returned to her office and checked his file again. He was seventy-nine with no close relatives. No one had visited him in three years. He was not a diabetic, but the nursing home did not keep very precise records of the amount of insulin used. With any luck, no one would know and no one would care.

She filled a syringe with insulin and, making her rounds, stopped at his room. It took a few seconds to find a vein and inject the insulin. She kept some pressure on the puncture site until she was sure there would be no bruising, then left him.

In the morning, the PSW found him dead. The doctor signed the death certificate as natural causes. No autopsy was felt necessary. The undertaker took care of all the formalities. The body was removed, and no one heard anything further. A distant relative eventually came to collect his belongings, which had been boxed up and left in the basement.

The night following Jim's death, Max looked at her with a raised eyebrow. The wires had been removed from his jaw. He sang a few bars of Edith Piaf's song, which they both liked. "Non, Je ne regrette rien." He smiled. She smiled. "Rien de rien."

"Tonight we should celebrate *le Bon Dieu* by considering the soul and the body. Clearly, the body is not the soul, the essence of humanity. The body can function to some extent when the soul is gone, like Bob and Jim."

"So that begs the question 'What is the soul?'"

"I once read a very amusing article in a very clever little magazine called *The Journal of Irreproducible Results*. They were trying to measure the soul. They took a dozen Church of England clerics, weighed them carefully, then ground them up and reweighed them. The weight was the same, which showed that either the Church of England clerics had no soul or that the soul was weightless. As the computer boys continue to shrink everything down, eventually, all knowledge will be on a small microchip."

"Really?"

"So maybe the soul is a few atoms. Socrates believed that in the womb, we knew everything, but we lost that knowledge when we were delivered into the world. All learning was simply an attempt to regain that knowledge, maybe floating in dark matter."

"That is way over my head."

"Mine too. I am rambling. Heidegger's concept that past, present, and future are nonlinear but all jumbled up usually makes sense to me but sometimes not. Anyway, I certainly agree with him that we are 'thrown into this world.' Have you started to look for your paramour?"

"Oh, Max, should I? He has probably pickled his brains with booze. What good would it do to find him?"

"*Cherie*, if you don't try, you may regret it forever. I once heard it said that the saddest words in the English language are *it might have been*. There must be a list of doctors somewhere. If he still has a license, he must still have a brain. Search for him on Google."

A few days later, Max broached the subject again. "You have looked?"

"Yes. I think I have found him. He works at a walk-in clinic in Chicago."

"*Eh bien*. Then you must find the courage to contact him."

"I know, I know. I will do it tomorrow."

"Tomorrow is another day, Scarlett."

"Yes, Rhett." And they both laughed.

"There is something else. You know that during the day I talk to other inhabitants of this establishment."

"Yes."

"Maisie has bed sores on her bottom, and her heels hurt all the time. I know you ladies try to turn her frequently, but she is not getting better, and she does not want to go to a hospital for treatment. One of her friends had a big operation for that. It did not work, and she died in agony anyway. When I was talking to her, she told me that she prays for the good Lord to take her soon. She looks forward to passing on to a better place."

"Max, you are not—?"

"*Non. Non Cherie*. Of course not. That would be asking more than anyone has any right to ask of you."

A couple of nights later, Maisie died in her sleep. Max simply raised an eyebrow when he next saw Sheila. She did not respond at all.

Chapter 9

Oh, What Is Death?

"Max, I can't talk to anyone else. On your suggestion, I helped Maisie on her way to that place of peace she wanted to go. But I don't know how I feel or how I should feel. I know I am the fourth horsemen of the Apocalypse, the rider on a pale horse, but am I bringing peace or conflict? Is this surcease or murder? Help me understand. It is not that I have much to live for myself. Sometimes I feel the answer is to curse God and die."

"Don't do it before I quit this vale of tears. Without you, I would be asking the guy who rows across the river Styx how much the fare is. You are the only bright star I have in this whole darkening world."

"God help us! Two lost souls in a leaky lifeboat in this dying city of Detroit in a civilization that has lost its way. No more glad mornings."

"Don't give up, Sheila. Think rather, 'Blessed on this morn to be alive' or 'Some work of noble note may yet be done, not unbecoming men that strove with gods.'"

"I wish I could believe that, Ulysses Max.

> And sitting well in order smite the sounding furrows.
> It may be we shall touch the Happy Isle
> And see the great Achilles whom we knew."

She broke down in tears. "Oh, Max. My Achilles was Dr. John. I threw it all away trying to save one child."

Max looked on helplessly as she wept soundlessly, her shoulders heaving, her face in her hands. What was there to say? He ventured, "'that rugged cross was my cross too.' A blameless person, tortured and crucified, our greatest story."

"But I was not born to be the Christ, Max. Why me? I can't take all the sins of the world on my shoulders."

"Why anyone? Heidegger's *das nichts* are here for us all."

"Max, I often feel like taking a few pills and then the hurt and the loneliness would be over—a blast of fentanyl and it's all gone."

"Seneca the Stoic said life is bearable because you always have that option. So we can struggle up the hill to what? Heaven or our own crucifixion. Or rather, you can. I am simply waiting at the station for the train to oblivion. 'Ah, make the most of what we yet may spend, before we too unto the dust descend.' Heidegger said that we often forget to live. To open my window and look into the garden would be enough for him. But you, you need something more in your life, 'something missing, something lost behind the ranges.'"

"Oh, Max. I am 'in the Barrens, the pass that betrayed them.'"

"Ah yes, Kipling, is it not?

> Where the wolverine tumbles their packs from the camp,
> And the grave mound we made them.
> Hear now the Song of the Dead.

"Sheila, there is no guilt. You are not the angel of death but the angel of mercy. God in his infinite wisdom has sent you here to look after the suffering and the dying. Helping them on their way to their eternal rest is an act of mercy."

"Even without their consent?"

"My problem, Sheila, my greatest fear is that my mind dies before my body. The body which remains after my mind has gone with the best will in the world and the best care in the world, which no one can provide other than potentially a Japanese robot, will be abused. Everyone will heave a sigh of relief when this useless husk of a body dies. I lie awake at night thinking of the horror of it. There is no way I want that. The problem is that by the time I know it is time for me to pass on, my mind is gone and I am unable to make that decision to ask for release. Even in Belgium, Holland, and Switzerland where such requests are legal, they really have not answered that question, at least not officially. *Das Man*, society, who tells us who we are and who we should be, is silent on this."

"But why? It is obviously a major problem. Everyone surely recognizes that?"

"So you would think. Heidegger says that death defines our time in life, but no one wants to talk about it. Perhaps it is because if you admit that you will inevitably die, you equally have to recognize that you are not in fact completely in control of your life."

"That there is a higher being? a force? a god?"

"I don't know. One of the best interpretations I ever read was from John the Scot who wrote in the early Middle Ages that God does not know himself, in other words, that God is an unknown, unknowable force. That is one explanation. It may force people into strange beliefs. Perhaps they are tortured by their own guilt. Who knows what demons lurk in the depths of the soul.

"Keep mama alive when she has no brain and when without a machine to inflate her lungs she couldn't breathe. I mean, how can anyone seriously think that mama is alive in there? And yet one endlessly reads in the newspapers of some last-minute court challenge where some really unthinking judge, and there are a whole lot of unthinking ones out there, signs an order preventing the hospital from switching off the machines. I have nothing against the ruling of the judge if the judge and the family pay to keep the machines going, the whole cost of the hospital, nursing, IVs, and all the rest. But of course they never do. It is some poor nameless taxpayer who pays for this lunacy."

"How will it all end, Max?"

"God knows. What happens when the state runs out of money? The US simply prints more money because the US dollar is the reserve currency. But what do the bankrupt countries like Greece and Spain do? I don't know. Are their hospitals full of dead people on ventilators?"

"A dead person on a ventilator, what a horrible thought."

"But it's true. If you have no brain function, you are certainly no longer human, whatever that is, and no one has ever defined exactly what a human is. They are less alive than a flower in a water vase. The cut flower does not need a machine to push the water up into it, and some cut flowers can even sprout roots."

"Oh God, Max. This is so depressing. Let's talk about something else."

"You are right. I can't remember who said it, but I think it is true. 'I have spent most of my life trying to be what others expected me to be, only to discover that in the end no one cared.' So for now, I try to think differently. 'One moment in annihilation's waste, one moment of the well of life to taste.' Let me have another drink and add up my blessings and a rather belated 'gather ye rosebuds while ye may' or 'this grey spirit yearning in desire to follow knowledge like a sinking star.'"

"You do that, Max. I must go help the others. See you tomorrow."

Chapter 10

Dreams Die Hard

"Max, I had another terrible dream last night. I was back in that tiny room with these three animals raping that little boy. I had a KA-BAR in my hand. I don't know if you have ever seen one. It is the original marine fighting knife. It is seven inches long and wickedly sharp. The rapist turned to me, pulling himself out of the little boy. He turned so quickly he ran onto the knife, and I woke up. The knife went into him. I have had that dream, that nightmare so many times. That moment was the end of my life."

"Dreams are strange, Sheila. No one knows what they are or where they come from. We do know that if you are prevented from dreaming, you go mad. After my first child, I used to have this nightmare frequently. He had fallen into the water. I was swimming down to get him, but he was sinking faster than I could swim. He got deeper and deeper, and then I woke up. I never had it again after the birth of my second child, or rather my wife's second child. I eventually got suspicious and had DNA testing done, but it did turn out that they actually were mine."

"Oh, Max. You are kidding. You thought that?"

"I forget the figures I heard somewhere: 24 percent of the kids do not have the fathers they think they have."

"Twenty-four percent? That can't be true."

"That was from an MGTOW, a Men Going Their Own Way YouTube site, so the figures are likely fudged, but still. Think of the numbers."

"Is that why you have no contact with them? You thought that?"

"No. They were pretty much grown up by the time I became suspicious. They were the modern, standard kids that are every ambitious father's nightmare. Try this college, drop out, and then try the next. Clever, really clever, but no ambition, no desire to work hard, and no vision of the future. Eventually it became clear we had nothing in common, so we drifted apart. And I have not seen or heard from them for years, and I don't particularly feel any need to see them. All that would do is remind me of my own foolishness for falling in love with their mother, who was not exactly faithful to me.

> I closed and drew for my love's sake
> That now is false to me
> And I slew the Riever of Tarrant Moss
> And set Dumeny free."

"Max, how sad, how terribly, terribly sad."

"Whenas I leaned on a lad's belief

And not on my naked blade.
And I slew a thief and an honest thief
For the sake of a worthless maid.

"I was so naive. But you know, recently I have been thinking that while I used to blame them, I now wonder if I was not equally to blame. I was young, or not so young but full of myself. I thought I was another genius. Socrates, Plato, Aristotle, and John the Scot all rolled into one. I was publishing my writings, which I thought would turn philosophy on its head, appearing as a talking head whenever I got a chance. Rushing off to one useless conference after another where I spoke to my equally self-important peers.

And when I came home, I just wanted a drink and to think, to think deep thoughts, which, in retrospect, were meaningless because I knew no quantum mechanics, robotics, or AI. Maybe I had no time for *les pauvre enfants*, the poor kids. Maybe I was just so goddamn selfish. Maybe if I had spent any time with the poor little things, it all might have turned out better. I don't like to think about it, but maybe I ruined the lives of these kids. But it's all gone, water under the bridge.

Gone, Gone, Gone with Thebes the Golden.
Don't tell me now I didn't give you warning.

Mon Dieu, Sheila, maybe I was a monster."

"Well, what can you do, Max, curse God and die? 'Winter has come and gone, but grief returns with the revolving year.' Water under the bridge! 'Gone, Gone, Gone with Lost Atlantis.'"

"*C'est vrai*. True! *Oui*! *C'est tout fini*. Too late. Anyway, we were talking about dreams, or rather, nightmares. When I used to travel a fair amount to lecture in Asia or Europe, the traveling salesman I got to know taught me to take sleeping pills and melatonin for the first couple of nights I was in a new time zone. The third night, you stop, and then you catch up on REM sleep. You know, rapid eye movement sleep, the dreaming sleep, the sleep which the sleeping pills suppress, and you have nightmares all night. The recurrent one I used to get was I was alone on a flat, empty plain. The light was strange, like early evening, and there was this incredible sense of menace. Nothing ever happened, but I knew something terrifying was coming, and then I would waken up. That was the only time I ever had that nightmare. Those are the only two dreams I remember. All the others I would forget as soon as I woke up even if I tried in the night to write down fragments. What I had written never made any sense in the morning."

"Oh yes, what was John Milton's poem about his dream of his dead wife? 'She inclined to me. I woke, and day turned into night.'"

"Bravo, Sheila! How many people nowadays have even heard of Milton?"

"Or the prince of Denmark? 'To sleep. To sleep. Perchance to dream.' But these demented old people I deal with, what do they dream of, or do they?"

"Who knows? They still have brain activity. But do they sense anything? Is some part still active, locked in a tiny cell deep in the brain, like the prisoner of Chalon?"

"One hears stories of those in a coma for years who woke up."

"Yes, yes, one hears. But I don't remember anyone who experienced it actually writing about it or describing it, whether or not they dreamed. I don't think so. Think of brainwashing. People go mad if placed in an isolation tank for a few hours."

"Maybe the ones in coma can hear?"

"If so, they should be able to show that with a functional MRI machine, and someone must have thought of that. But I have not heard anything or read anything, so I doubt it."

"So these demented old people in here, what are they thinking about?"

"Maybe of demons, especially the aggressive ones who fight off the nurse trying to clean up their incontinence. Maybe they are like Francis Thompson, running away from some imaginary daemon.

> I fled him down the nights and down the days.
> I fled him down the arches of the years.
> I fled him down the labyrinthine ways of my own mind."

"Do you really believe that?"

"No. I think they are mostly on hindbrain function only, the ancient lizard brain, when nothing above the brainstem is working, like the neck-righting reflex in a cat."

"What is that?"

"If you cut the head off a cat and throw it out of a window, there are reflexes in the neck so that it can twist in the air and land on its feet."

"Really, you're joking!"

"No. I am sure I read that years ago. I am sure it is like pain impulse, which is still there in people who are semiconscious."

"So even these poor demented people still have pain from their bed sores?"

"I would think so because the nerves are still there, and pain is a very primitive system. I mean, if you touch a hot stove, you jerk your hand away immediately. You don't think about it. Your body does it for you. So pain impulses and reactions occur without conscious thought. Someone said that the only reason you feel pain is to remind yourself not to do that action again."

"God, so they have pain. I wish they did not. We try so hard to turn them every couple of hours to relieve the pressure on the skin to stop the bed sores, but it is so difficult. There are so many of them, and there is never enough staff."

"Yes, an impossible problem. And even if they get surgery to fix the bed sore, it is bound to come back sometime in a week or a month or a year."

"And the smell of the incontinence—even we nurses never quite get used to it. The families who visit almost vomit, which is why so many avoid visiting. They blame us, not knowing that we might have cleaned the patient half an hour before. Sometimes they are incontinent again before we even get out of the room. It is misery for the family, the patient, and the staff."

"A labor of Sisyphus, which only ends in death. 'Out, out brief candle, lighting the way to dusty death.' I am sure some patients and their families would be very happy if someone blew out that candle."

"I know that, Max. We all know. But it is illegal in this country."

"In most countries, I think. But I am not sure how closely they monitor the situation in Europe, and I think the families there are a bit more realistic about life and death."

"It is all very strange. Some people and places are talking about fourth trimester abortion, basically letting a living, breathing baby die, and yet at the other end of the spectrum, we struggle to keep the mostly dead alive. Why? The dead husk of a chrysalis."

"It has always been that way for children. The Spartans used to expose the children they did not want on the hillside if they felt the child did not measure up. Old people? I don't know what they did with them. Maybe very few lived to be old. I heard, and I am sure it is not true, that during a really bad winter with no food, the Eskimos used to eat Grandma. The long pig they called it. In India, the wives of the rulers were burned on his funeral pyre, suttee. I was never sure why. Was it to make sure they did not poison him? Or was it so they could not plot against the new king? So how can it possibly be a crime against humanity if you help some of these poor demented, unwanted people into that good night?"

"I know, it makes no sense, but I am afraid. People have been jailed for accusations of mercy killings. I have no wish to be a martyr."

"Yes. Social mores don't necessarily make any intellectual sense, so be very very careful, Sheila. The families are the dangerous ones. They never visit for years. But when Grandma dies, they have this sense of guilt and look around for someone to blame about something, anything, to assuage their guilt."

"Some of the families who visit complain too, but you are right. The ones who come often know of the difficulties we have keeping the utterly dependent cleaned, turned, and fed. If they have done it themselves at home, they know just how difficult it is. But even then, some who know just how difficult it is still complain."

"Yes. The Western way of death really should be rethought. It is OK if the patient wants to fight against death, but the family fighting it on behalf of the patient who either does not want life or is not aware of it makes no sense. This is a major societal problem, and no one is considering it. Well, maybe Japan is. But no, I think that they are just deferring the decision with their nurse robots. They even have robots who act as children to amuse the very old who have no grandchildren of their own. But that is really just kicking the can down the road. It is not really making a decision. Have you ever been to Japan, Sheila?"

"No, I never had any desire to do so."

"I lectured at universities in Tokyo and Osaka a few times. I loved it. The Japanese gardens, serene and beautiful, not the regimented, military appearance of Versailles or Fontainebleau. They are natural, everything perfectly placed. Especially to go there in April in sakura time when the cherry blossom is flowering. It lasts a few magical days. What a difference! There they celebrate the transient fleeting beauty of life. They had four hundred years of civil war. All the young samurai died in battle by the thousands. The sakura time celebrates their brief life. I have not been there for years and alas never will again.

>No more we stop to see, pretty cherry blossoms.
>No more we, underneath the tree,
>looking at the sky. Sayonara, goodbye.

"You should go there someday at sakura time, Sheila."

"Maybe I will someday, Max. The transient beauty of life? Not really a Western concept, is it?"

"Well, I am not so sure. How about,

>Or like the snowfall in the river
>One moment white then gone forever.
>Or like the Borealis race
>That flit ere you can point the place.
>Or like the rainbow's lovely form
>Aye vanishing amid the storm."

"Perhaps you are right, Max,

>The hand of the reaper
>Takes the ears that are hoary

> But the voice of the weeper
> Wails manhood in glory.

But now I had better make my rounds. Perhaps you are right. Maybe one poor sick, demented old man with awful bed sores will pass on tonight."

"Was it Hope Grant, the English general, who said that 'death is merely opening the door to another room'? I hope so. Not that it matters. 'The paths of glory lead but to the grave.' We don't get out of this one alive. Good night, Sheila."

Chapter 11

Tomorrow and Tomorrow

"Max, if you tell me again not to worry my pretty little head, I won't bring you any Armagnac for a week."

"*Pardonne moi*! Clearly, you are serious, Sheila. Unfortunately serious philosophical debate gives me *mal de tete*, a headache. It always did, even as a young man. So like a true French intellectual, I turned my back on Michel de Montaigne who made thought easy and logical and instead made things utterly incomprehensible, then when no one understood what I was saying, obviously I was a genius, the master. Then they would listen to me."

"All gobbledygook?"

"*Oui*. As much as possible, we would spend hours when I was a student in Paris on the Left Bank of the Seine where we thought we were with Sartre at the next table accompanied by Simone or maybe bohemians or communists or revolutionaries. Che was our idol. We sat in these awful crowded little cafes with their rickety tables drinking foul cold coffee and pretending that we were solving the problems of existentialism—life and death, freedom to choose, and the endless mindless litany."

"Be serious for a moment, Max. If I am the bringer of death, am I doing wrong? I have helped four people in this old age home on their way to eternity. It is not clear to me whether I should feel guilty or not. Sometimes I think I do, but not very often."

"I should not worry too much. Angst does not help the world go round unless you are a teenager who knows nothing but thinks he knows everything and has heard the word *anomie* but does not understand what it means."

"What does it mean?"

"It was Durkheim who coined it. It means a lack of social ethic or rapid changes in standards or values of society, a bit like what is happening today. What is socially acceptable to say today might get you crucified tomorrow."

"Talking about being crucified, in the Bible it says 'thou shalt not kill.'"

"The Bible says many things, including not coveting thy neighbor's goods, and yet everyone does."

"They do?"

"Yes, they do. It is the temptation of all humans to live at the expense of someone else. I think it was the American Walter Williams who said this about farmers wanting subsidies: 'If he puts a gun to my head asking for money, he would go to jail. Instead he covets or want my goods or my money and does so legally by keeping voting in politicians who use the Law to take it from me.' They call this coveting or stealing taxation.

"And thou shalt not kill, well, maybe. Tell that to these wonderful ideologues Rachel Carson and Chairman Mao and good old Marx, the greatest killers in the world's history. They killed millions, with the best intentions, I am sure. That bunch killed so many people that they make Adolf Hitler look like Mr. Nice Guy, a minor player in the extermination league. Or the benevolent Pol Pot, who killed one-third of the population of his whole country. For him, starvation was too easy. He had them beaten to death in the name of socialism. And you have helped four people on their way, five if you include your Afghan rapist."

"You make it sound all so inconsequential."

"Because it is in the great scheme of things. We all die. Disraeli said that 'youth is a blunder; manhood a struggle, and old age a regret.' It is not the fact of but the manner of our death that matters. I like Kipling's story about the letter written by the Roman general after he lost a battle. 'The swords await at the tent door to give me the death I gave to Gratian. Therefore I, your General and your Emperor, send you free and honorable dismissal.' Great words. Or Group Captain Oates."

"Who was he?"

"When the explorer Scott was going to the South Pole, or rather coming back from it, one of his band, Group Captain Oates, got frostbite so badly he had difficulty walking. He knew he was slowing down the others to the extent that they would all die. One night, he walked out of their tent into a blizzard. He said, 'I am going outside. I may be a little time.' They all knew he was walking to his death. *Que hombre*, what a man!"

"What happened to the others?"

"They all died too, I think, within ten miles of their food cache, but they left written records. No one remembers the other names, but everyone knows of Captain Oates."

"But nowadays, no one knows of him, and in any event, that was a personal decision, like that French policeman recently who gave himself to some terrorist in exchange for the hostages. When the terrorist killed him, all France went on about how much they honored him, but within a few weeks, the city council in Marseilles refused to name a street after him."

"Yes, I suppose you are right. Only the waiting angel knows or remembers. But decision-making is what is difficult. Suppose your brain was gone and you were incapable of making that decision, or suppose your brain is OK but your body is so sick that you no longer have the strength to do the deed?"

"This is not a decision society is prepared to face."

"But it is one that doctors quietly face every day. It is only some families that fight with the doctor's recommendations. Most, I hear, accept the advice. But you are correct. Nothing is written down. If it is not written, then society does not make that decision. Look at Socrates. He had ample time to leave Athens, but he decided to stay and drink his hemlock with his friends around him. Or like the Japanese. In seppuku, you can open your own belly, but then your second is authorized to cut off your head. So think of yourself as a hara-kiri helper."

"So I shouldn't feel bad?"

"You are human. Nothing is ever perfect. We are all going to feel bad about something. Life sucks, and then you die. 'Into this universe and why not knowing whither.'"

"Yes, I know the rest of that verse. 'And out of it, like water on the waste, willy nilly flowing.'"

"Except for these Soviet communist morons who diverted the two rivers willy-nilly flowing into the Aral Sea, and now it is effectively the Aral desert. Another triumph of good old Marx."

"You loathe Marx. You are always slagging him."

"When you think of the misery that evil old man is responsible for, he is head and shoulders the most evil person who ever lived. There is no one, absolutely no one, in his league of monstrosity. He is Leviathan or the beast in Revelations. The brain worm he released has infected generations of poor, simple, slightly stupid students; and these useless idiots help provide cover for the utterly malevolent.

"Yada! Yada! Yada! I am sorry, Sheila. I am getting carried away with my rant. I am sure you have heard me say it all before."

"That's OK. Now tell me how you really feel about Marx. Don't hold back."

"Let us not discuss that piece of filth. It leaves a bad taste in my mouth, a vast desire to go back in time and drown the son of a bitch at birth. The fall of the Berlin Wall indicated that socialism had failed, and yet all Western governments seek to expand, not retract, which is what they should have done. It's crazy. The road to serfdom, socialism, leads inevitably to totalitarianism. But let us talk about something happy. Have you been able to track down the love of your life?"

"Oh, Max, should I? I have a new life here, quiet and calm. I read the books you suggest, and I am learning more poetry and a little French. When I talk to you, it's like a private seminar at a high-level university, an almost Epicurean existence, I think."

"Yes, indeed. In a way, you are living as Epicurus suggested. In a sense, all these young people, these millennials, are too. They just don't know it. The aim of modern life is not only to be harmless but to announce publicly that you are harmless and that you and your life have no meaning. But surely, Sheila, you want more.

> As though to breathe were life.
> Life piled on life were all too little."

"Ulysses again. Maybe I should look for the Taoist way?"

"When you are my age, possibly. But at your age, no! You want 'sitting well in order, smite the sounding furrows.'"

"Max, I did that with alcohol and drugs and sex. It was fun at the time. I loved it. But now? I still remember waking up in the gutter lying in a pool of my own vomit. The 'sounding furrows' did not work out too well for me."

"I am sorry, Sheila. An old man dreaming dreams of what never was.

> Yet Ah that spring should vanish with the rose,
> and youth's sweet scented manuscript should close.

Sometime I dream that I was Roland of the chanson fame, or Francois Villon, the troubadour. Realistically, I would have been more like Vercingetorix; the fool who got all his people killed fighting Caesar."

"The attempted liberator?"

"Liberate them from what? Rome offered civilization, and they wanted their mud huts in the forest. After Rome fell, these idiots did not even know how to make bricks. Can you imagine? They went from central heating to no bricks. Freedom! OK, maybe. You remember the poem,

> The cry of those you humor
> Ah, slowly to the light.
> Why brought ye us from bondage
> Our loved Egyptian night.

"Look around you at the glories of Western civilization. Did you know the Japanese were so impressed that they almost switched officially to English language? And now we have these university and political relativist morons who want to toss it all away. All cultures have the same value? A mud hut is as good as the Parthenon? Give me a break! Or better, give me another drink."

"OK. Enough with the sorrow already. Now I have got to get back to my work, Max. I will see you tomorrow night."

"Sheila, a` demain. I look forward to it."

Chapter 12

PTSD

"How goes it, Sheila?"

"Not good. My PTSD is still there, Max. I don't know if I will ever be completely rid of it."

"What happened?"

"I acted like a total moron this afternoon. Jeez, I can't believe it. I was coming out of my bank, and there in front of me was the same man that Doc John saved me from at the hospital in Kandahar. It was either the same Shaheed or his identical twin—the same flat hat, the same long white nightshirt, the same bulky black overcoat, the same beard, and the same staring eyes. I was terrified. Instinctively I threw myself back inside the bank door and dove to the floor against the inside wall of the bank.

"I cowered there with my legs drawn up into a ball. And then the Shaheed came in, looked curiously at me on the floor, and went to the bank counter. I felt such an idiot. Everyone in the bank was staring at me like I was a crazy woman. I suppose they are right. I am. I thought the worst of my PTSD had gone away, but that was a pretty terrible flashback."

"That must have been really terrifying, Sheila."

"God, isn't there anywhere I can go in the US where I won't run into people dressed like Shaheed's?"

"Don't let anyone hear you say that, Sheila. If you said that in Europe, they would lock you up as a hate criminal or a Nazi or something; and if you say it anywhere near a university in this country, you are liable to get stoned."

"What is the US coming to? I thought we had a First Amendment enshrining free speech. Is it really back to the Dark Ages? 'They stoned Stephen outside the walls of Jerusalem.'"

"Sheila, Sheila, the American experiment was such an unlikely concept brought into being by an unlikely group of men. It is surprising that it lasted as long as it did. In France, they change the constitution every decade or two. There is no legal status of free speech in the whole of Europe. Britain has given up its common law heritage. The Magna Carta was signed in 1215. 'Trumpets in the marshes round the eyot of Runnymede.' But eight hundred years later, 'the silver snarling trumpets' have fallen silent. In the last twenty years, the Brits have thrown away that glorious heritage that civilized half the world.

"Canada has this insane constitution that can be changed at will by a bunch of unelected, none-too-smart judges who are political appointees. No, Sheila, it is over. You were in the military. You know what it means to run for cover. An old guy like me can almost say what he likes. They excuse us because they say we are senile, and we have no job from which they can have us fired. But you, keep your head down and your mouth shut. Otherwise the thought police, the Stasi, the KGB, or the *mutaween*—the religious police—will be coming for you."

"You mean I went to Afghanistan and all these young US soldiers died so that we could bring that culture and their religious police here?"

"I am sure that was not the intention, but it certainly has become the reality."

"Then the long night of horror has come to America."

"*Mais oui*, get used to it. The US dream is vanishing. 'Out out brief candle.'"

"I guess Doc John was right. Read the literature and poetry of the past and try to ignore the present."

"Yes, just as people have always done, world without end. Those brief flowers of the Enlightenment, freedom and Western culture are wilting and dying.

> Oh love they die in yon rich sky
> They faint on field and hill and river
> Our echoes roll from soul to soul,
> and grow forever and forever.

"Except they don't. Instead it is 'the horns of Efland, dying, dying, dying.'

> So no more 'glad morning of my days.
> No! No more glad mornings."

"Oh, Max, talking to you leaves me so depressed. Maybe you should tell me lies for a change."

"*Mais bien sur*, of course I can do that. 'Grow old along with me; the best is yet to be.'"

"I was thinking of *Pippa's Song*.

> The year's at the spring,
> And the day's at the morn;
> God's in his heaven
> All's right with the world!"

"Yes, you could certainly dream of Christ reborn.

> I have seen him cow a thousand men
> On the hills of Galilee.
> They whined as he walked out calm between
> With his eyes like the grey of the sea.
> If they think they have slain our goodly Frere
> They are fools eternally.
> I have seen him eat of the honeycomb
> Since they nailed him to the tree."

"I wish, Max. The resurrection. On that happy note, let me go and change some incontinent people."

"Ah, Sheila, 'twas glorious on that morn to be alive,' 'better to have loved and lost than never to have loved at all.'"

"Yeah, yeah. Keep telling me that. Maybe it is even true. See you tomorrow, Max."

Chapter 13

Götterdämmerung

"Ah, Sheila, bonsoir, good to see you, and *merci bien* for the Armagnac. Here are a couple of hundred bucks to cover the cost."

"Max, you should not drink so much. I feel guilty bringing it to you."

"A short life but a merry one, Sheila. As the Romans would say, 'Eat, drink and be merry for tomorrow we die.' Or,

> Come fill the cup and in the fire of spring
> The winter garment of repentance fling
> The bird of time has but a little way to fly
> And lo, the bird is on the wing."

"I hear you, Max, but the next verse is also true.

> Indeed the idols I have loved so long
> Have done my credit in men's eyes much wrong,
> Have drowned my honor in a shallow cup
> And sold my reputation for a song."

"Bravo, Sheila. *Tres bien*. My reputation, if I ever had one,

> Gone with the wind, flung roses,
> Roses riotously with the throng"

"But, Max, that's me,

> Desolate and sick of an old passion,
> When I awoke and found the dawn was grey.

What is happening to the world? Was it always so full of pain?"
"If you believe Hobbes, it probably it always was. 'Nasty, brutish and short,' as the poet said, and it makes sense.

> Who would remember Helen's face
> Lacking the halo of spears?
> Who formed Christ but Herrod and Caesar?"

"'Violence has been the source of all the world's value.' You mean, was there ever a glad morning? I don't think so. Like François Villon, 'If I ruled the world, every man would be as free as a bird.' Not very likely. Utopia, the ultimate dream of all mankind, is simply not achievable. It has been said that 'utopia exists across a sea of blood and you never get there. It is just one more execution away.' Look at all the attempts at socialism, including my poor France, another revolution run by lawyers. All revolutions are run by lawyers, and all end the same way. They hang everyone, and then they in turn are hung by a greater monster than they were.

"Robespierre, Danton, and Marat, all lawyers, all eventually monsters. No matter with what good intentions they started, it ended in a blood bath, the terror, just like Lenin, another lawyer, and his Red Terror. But it is hard, very hard, to proclaim a resistance against these overarching messianic ideologies. I once heard the Englishman Roger Scruton say that his Conservative battle cry would be 'Hesitate!' Not something people would rally around."

"Are you really a Conservative?"

"I hate labels, Sheila. The left, led by people like Adorno of the Frankfurt School, simply take a word and twist it to mean the opposite. Like Humpty Dumpty, 'a word means what I say it means,' like social justice. Justice is either justice or it is not. They call Nazis right wing, and yet the name *Nazi* is national socialist. Hitler and Mussolini were socialists. Fascism and Nazism were socialism. Lenin sent a message of congratulations to Mussolini when his Black shirts took over Italy. If you really want a label, I suppose I am a Jeffersonian Trotskyist."

"Are they not opposites?"

"Yes and no. Trotsky once wrote that his goal was to increase the power of man over nature and decrease the power of man over man. Jefferson was not so different. 'A wise and frugal government, which shall restrain men from injuring one another, which shall leave them otherwise free to regulate their own pursuits of industry and improvement, and shall not take from the mouth of labor the bread it has earned.' That's me, that's what I want.

"Clint Eastwood spoke for me in that movie of his when he said, 'Get off my lawn.' Just leave me alone. Rather than these slimy politicians, give me a good old war lord every time, like Julius Caesar. He executed no one, other than poor silly Vercingetorix, who deserved it for leading his revolt against Caesar. 'And the blood and iron on which you pin your faith fell as nothing before the spirit of man.' Actually he gave him a hard time at Alesia, one of the few times Caesar actually had to think."

"Weren't all the Roman emperors' bloodthirsty monsters?"

"No, no, very few unless you went to war against Rome. I liked Caesar's books, especially *De Bello Gallico*, his day journal of his wars in Western Europe. I actually googled it, and a book written more than a thousand years ago is available from Amazon for about twenty bucks, quite amazing. It is still worth reading, to see what sort of a man he was. Sometimes I think I could have followed a man like that."

"You, Max the philosopher?"

"Me, Max Labienus the warrior, his ramrod, or me and Marcus Aurelius."

"Another Roman?"

"The last great emperor. Died in AD 180. He spent his life on the frontier fighting off the Germanic tribes coming westward. His book *Meditations* is still definitely worth reading. It is actually on audio books for five dollars. His son Commodus gave up defending the empire and returned to Rome. Two hundred years later, Rome fell, but that was likely one of the pivotal moments."

"Really? Rome depended on one man?"

"No. It is never that simple. But one man is a symbol. Trade resulted in the introduction of malaria, which spread up along the trade routes from Africa. Then there was welfare, currency debasement, and all the other usual suspects."

"I think you are going to tell me more than I actually need to know. Is this the story of the downfall of the West?"

"Götterdämmerung? The twilight of the gods, yes. The process is fairly well-known. The Chinese have described it best. They describe it in four stages endlessly repeating throughout history. For them, it has happened five times before. The age of the hero begins the process. He pulls his tribe from the dirt and foulness of chaos to establish a civilization. The golden age follows when everything flourishes—art, science, and literature. Men believe in honesty, honor, courage, and patriotism; and women believe in themselves and their destiny."

"What does that mean?"

"Think of the British Empire—these tough women who went out with their men to the ends of the earth, afraid of nothing, and had their children there. The advice when being raped was to 'lie back and think of England,' knowing that if they lived and could tell their story, their men would come, hot and angry, and exact a terrible vengeance on the rapist and his clan. That is a little different from the tender me-tooers of today or these gutless wonders in Germany and Sweden who won't protect their women."

"And the other ages?"

"The merchant age follows, when people only care about money. The ruling class becomes effete. They despise honesty, courage, and patriotism—anything good and wholesome. Currency is debased to pay for welfare, bread, and circuses. Real wages drop. Women debase themselves, losing any sense of honor and responsibility, and stop having babies. This is followed by the age of chaos when it all falls apart. The rot begins from within, and then the barbarians stroll over the undefended walls, and everything descends into chaos. And oh, yes, it has happened in the West also. Think of the civilizations of Greece, Rome, Byzantium, Spain, and now Britain—five fallen civilizations just like in China."

"So where are we at present on this wheel of disaster?"

"Perfectly obvious, the late merchant age. There is no longer any belief in ourselves, our culture, our past, our religion, our honor, or our dignity. Everything is becoming progressively debased. Look at the joke of modern art. How can anyone take that garbage seriously? Or modern music? The only deep satisfaction is the knowledge that the elites, those responsible, never ever survive the ensuing chaos of the Dark Ages."

"Dear God, Max, you really think it is as bad as that?"

"Look around you, Sheila. The current dying mainstream media is full of fake news. The universities and schools provide no education, or what they teach is either nonsense or frank lies. If you like to consider it, education has been totally taken over by the collectivists. It is completely centralized, so it provides a low-quality, standardized product and benefits very few people, only the administrators and the socialist politicians."

"What is this postmodernism I keep hearing about?"

"At its most basic when you break it down to its simplest, it is a hatred of competence, of anyone who is successful at anything. It is the mantra of the failure: 'It wasn't my fault that I failed. It was someone else who made me fail.' What they are teaching is equality of outcome—that if you are competent, you are evil and must be held back. Even the hard sciences are being corrupted. Look at this climate science drivel. It has nothing to do with science. Even the famous email scandal, which showed the world that they were lying, was essentially ignored by the media and the politicians who whitewashed it. They will not cherchez la femme."

"Look for the woman? What does that mean?"

"Sorry, Sheila. My Frenchness is showing. *Follow the woman* is our corruption of *cui bono*. 'Who benefits?' Someone always benefits, so the question is who? It is not too difficult when you think of it. Who benefits from this green rubbish, this disruption of Western manufacturing? And who gets paid to foment this disruption?"

"Aha!"

"Yes, aha indeed. A certain country does not screw up its own manufacturing at all and keeps its energy prices low, and who gets promotions and pensions?"

"I don't want to go there, Max. Goodness, look at the time. I have to get back to my work and see if my staff needs any help."

"Sheila, have a look at Jasmine at the end of the corridor. She is sick and feels so tired and unwell. She told me today that every night she prays she will not wake up in the morning. She says all her days are miserable, and she wishes they would end."

Sheila rolled her eyes, sighed, and left.

Chapter 14

Happiness

"Having a good evening, Max?"

"Why, thank you for asking, Sheila. *Mais non*, I am not. I was contemplating a wasted life."

"Whose? Mine or yours?"

"Mine. I thought I was clever, sitting with my friends on La Rive Gauche, the left bank of the Seine, in Paris in our little cafes with the terrible cold coffee, being revolutionaries, talking endlessly of this and that, about things we knew nothing of and understood less. Impressed with my ability to spout incomprehensible gobbledygook, I became a university professor of philosophy."

"Max Socrates educating youth?" said Sheila with a grin, having heard much of this gripping before.

"Educating the young on some concepts they barely understood, which, in retrospect, I also did not understand. As the poet says,

> Myself when young did eagerly frequent
> Teacher and saint. But evermore came out
> Of the same door as in I went.
> There was a door to which I found no key
> There was a veil past which I could not see.

"Nowadays it is perfectly clear that none of the philosophers ever truly had any understanding of reality. Giordano Bruno may have come closest when he wrote his paradox: 'We are surrounded by eternity, but there is a center from which all species come and return.' It is the AI and the robotics guys who are going to define reality. Their robots won't be able to function without an understanding of what reality actually is."

"So the engineers in reality know more about reality than the philosophers?"

"Yes, in both senses. It was realizing that that made me finally realize I had wasted my life teaching in France and here in the Ivy Leagues."

"A lot of *realize* and *reality* going on there."

"Yes, to realize that what I was teaching had as little to do with reality as the medieval 'how many saints can dance on the head of a pin?' No wonder so many philosophers were so unhappy. Poor Blaise Pascal, the cripple, wasting his prodigious mathematical talents trying to convince himself he was happy in his room on his own. Or Schopenhauer saying that 'only when he is alone is man really free.' Or Wittgenstein and Heidegger who likely both had Asperger's syndromes. Or Kierkegaard, terrified of death, which had taken all his siblings and took him too horribly. Or Rochefoucauld, the unrequited lover. The only happy one was David Hume."

"David Hume? I have not heard of him."

"Because he is too easy to understand and liked making money, a Scotsman who spent a lot of time in Paris, where he was popular. *Le Bon Davide*. He felt that if God existed, we should not be bothering him as he was likely busy."

"So what would you like to have done with your life?"

"I should have been an engineer. I have just been reading of the life of Isambard Kingdom Brunel. He did everything. He changed the face of England with his bridges, railroads, and tunnels. He built the first propeller-driven transatlantic steamship. He built clean, functional, portable hospitals for Florence Nightingale in the Crimean War. All that I knew about, but I did not know that he also built a vacuum-driven railroad. Can you believe it? One hundred fifty years ago, he built a high-speed vacuum system where the train could go at one hundred kilometers. His problem was that the seals for the system were made out of animal hides as there were no plastics, and of course, the rats ate the hides. It is only now that Elon Musk is considering building such a system in the US."

"He sounds like quite a man."

"Yes, and he died in his fifties. Or an engineer like Gustave Eiffel, who not only built the tower but also the Statue of Liberty in New York. Because he lived until his nineties, he built a huge body of bridges, viaducts, and buildings all over the world."

"Wasn't he involved in some sort of scandal?"

"I think so, something to do with the Panama Canal. But I think he outlived that. He must have been so proud looking back on his deathbed."

"Maybe, but I doubt that all successful people are happy."

"*Mai oui*, but what is it to be happy anyway? There are all sorts.

> Then let not what I cannot have
> My peace of mind destroy.
> While thus I sing I am a king
> Although a poor blind boy."

"Blind children? Did I not read something about that the other day?"

"Yes. They have recently developed genetically modified rice, Golden Rice. It is as much a breakthrough as when Norman Borlaug developed dwarf grains, which fed half the world. Someone wrote in a book I read that 'famine, the Third Horsemen of the Apocalypse, was spurring his black horse into action, when damn me, if the human race led by Norman Borlaug, had not ambushed him and shot the son of a bitch clean between the eyes.' If he developed it now, these idiots would try to prevent it from being planted."

"Eh? Why?"

"Because they do not understand genetic modification and think it is wrong. They do not know that everything we have is genetically modified, like horses, potatoes, almost all fruits. The problem is that these green people have had no scientific education, and this is really an ersatz religion for them, which has replaced the one they were never ever taught. This Golden Rice has vitamin A in it, which prevents vitamin-deprived children from going blind. Yet these fools have prevented it from being planted everywhere except in one Far East country."

"You mean that these people would rather see children go blind than allow it to be planted? How can they go to sleep at night knowing that they are responsible for this unspeakable cruelty?"

"I don't think that they have much difficulty. These are the same people who supported the gulags. They are happy to wade through a sea of blood in the name of their crazed ideology. Some of them, I am sure, are themselves simply poor blind children who do not recognize that they are being manipulated by others with a malevolent agenda."

"I was a poor blind girl, Max. To pay my father back for ignoring me and for my sisters looking down on me, I ended up dropping out of school and joining a commune, with free love and all, where I and a few other deluded idiots provided the free love for anyone who wanted it. Filthy accommodation, filthy food, but we kidded ourselves we were having a great time, free from the world."

"How did you get out of that?"

"After I got beaten up a few times by the leader of the commune, I eventually smartened up. I went to work as a cook at the up-country mining camps and even once at an asbestos mine in Northern Quebec. We were told it was not the type of asbestos that causes cancer, but I don't know if that was true. If in the next few years I don't get a mesothelioma, the cancer produced by one form of asbestos, I will know that they did not lie to us."

"A frightening thought."

"Well, you end up living with it. Eventually I saved enough money to go back to school. As I knew nothing, with virtually no education and my only work experience as a camp cook, I did not know what else to do with my life. I knew how to get laid, but as I was drunk or high much of the time, how good I was even at that I do not know. So I got a student loan and went to nursing school in Michigan. I did not know how I would possibly pay off that loan. And as the bill collectors kept hounding me, I eventually became a US citizen and joined the military as they paid nurses pretty well, and so I eventually ended up in Afghanistan."

"Ah, *ma pauvre*, at least you survived. Very brave!

> Out of the night that covers me
> Black as the pit from pole to pole
> I thank whatever gods there be
> For my unconquerable soul."

"I suppose that is one way of looking at it. Thanks, Max, for saying that, 'my unconquerable soul.' I wish. There's Jane at the door. I have to get back to work."

"Look for the man you once loved, Sheila. The saddest words in the entire world are *it might have been*."

Chapter 15

None Will Break Ranks

"God, Max, what an evening."

"Busy, Sheila?"

"Never-ending—incontinence, bed sores, and confused people wandering around. Sometimes I think I am living in one of these medieval paintings of hell."

"Yes. They had a pretty good idea of the reality of the situation in medieval Europe. But there were good times too, like the paintings of the Dutchman Bruegel."

"I don't think I have ever seen any."

"Look up YouTube. Everyone has seen his painting of the *Peasant Wedding* and the *Children's Games*, although they may not know that they are looking at a reproduction of a painting that is five hundred years old."

Sheila checked on her iPhone. "Yes, I see them. I never thought to do that before. You mean I can look at every painting ever done?"

"Maybe not all, but certainly most. Perhaps sometimes we should spend a few minutes looking at art. You will be amazed at how many partial reproductions of these paintings turn up in ads."

"Give me a list, and I will look them up. So looking at the *Peasant Wedding*, the medieval times, the Dark Ages were not so dark?"

"Yes. The Eastern Roman Empire lasted until 1450. Even in the West, Rome did not just suddenly disappear overnight. Boethius, the most famous philosopher of that age, was alive and writing at around AD

500, and his writings were well-known in the Middle Ages. In a way, he describes you. 'For in all adversity of fortune the worst sort of misery is to have been happy.' There is also something you should think about when you are looking for your lover. He also wrote, 'A man content to go to heaven alone will never go to heaven.'"

"Alone, yes, that currently is me, I guess. I thought I had found happiness and togetherness in Afghanistan."

"And why not? There is a saying; I forget from where, that 'there is no happiness so complete as that snatched from under the shadow of the sword.' Or there is a poem I vaguely remember.

> Some bold adventurers disdain.
> Still as they run they look behind.
> They hear a voice in every wind
> And snatch a fearful joy.

"That would describe you in that hellhole in Afghanistan."

"Yes, it would. Oh yes, a voice in the wind, and I did not listen. So what happened to Boethius?"

"Oh, the usual. Accused of a crime he did not commit, jailed and executed by the authorities."

"Pretty awful."

"The story of humanity. But look on the bright side. If he had not been tossed in jail, he would never have written the book, and the world would be a lesser place."

"A high price for Boethius."

"Yes. Again the story of humanity—rinse and repeat endlessly. Jesus Christ himself broke no Roman laws. Pontius Pilate, the Roman governor, made that clear when he washed his hands and said he 'was innocent of the blood of this just man.' But to keep the peace, he gave Jesus to the social justice warriors who accused him of hate speech and who insisted he be tortured and crucified. He never did appeal to Rome, which he could not have done anyway as he was not a citizen. I have a sneaking suspicion that if he had ever done so, Pilate would have sent him to Rome to stand trial there, just like St. Paul, who did claim Roman citizenship to protect himself from the same social justice mob."

"Social justice mob?"

"Oh yes. The same people existed then. As it is written, 'they stoned Stephen outside the walls of Jerusalem.' To avoid that fate, Paul appealed to Rome."

"Appealed to Rome?"

"Any citizen had that right. Can you imagine it in the whole Roman Empire? No Roman citizen could be tried against his consent by some Mickey Mouse local thug anywhere within the empire."

"I forget what happened to St. Paul."

"He got unlucky. Nero was the emperor, so he lost his legal case and was executed."

"Oh dear."

"Not as bad as it sounds. Because he was a citizen, they cut his head off, a hell of a lot better than being crucified or stoned to death. But he got to do a lot of preaching on the way to Rome. They were tough guys, these early Christians."

"It all sounds so awful."

"I know. The early Christian church was no better. It went from being a slave religion to the church militant. If it wasn't for the early church accepting the teachings of Duns Scotus and Thomas Aquinas, we would still be stuck, burning Giordano Bruno and John Huss. If only Islam had listened to Averroes, Ibn Rushd, the world would be a different and infinitely better place."

"I don't want to think about theology."

"Not so! You don't want to think about organized religions, not the concept of religion."

"There is a difference?"

"Oh yes, a very big difference. One is the belief in something. The other is the imperfect interpretation of that belief. And it can get pretty imperfect. Think of what has been happening in the Middle East for more than a thousand years. Men are killing each other on the basis of some minor point of doctrine they do not really understand, egged on by criminal clerics. The easiest way to think of religion is Kant's categorical imperative, which is simply to act as if God existed and do the right thing."

"But what is the right thing?"

"It is like pornography. You know it when you see it."

"Does it matter?"

"Yes, it does, absolutely. The West has lost its faith. Nietzsche said 'God is dead.' My compatriot Auguste Comte agreed but felt that the pomp and circumstance, the music, the rituals, and the gorgeous architecture would help people live day to day. He wanted a secular religion glorifying man."

"A bit presumptuous, perhaps?"

"Yes, sure. But why not? Comte did not call for the death of anyone. If more people had listened to him, it would have been certainly better than what Nietzsche predicted very accurately—that religion would be replaced by some other murderous movement, infinitely worse, like socialism and its eternal offshoot of social justice."

"You really think these silly kids are going to be a major problem?"

"Oh yes! Do not underestimate them. The Greens, the socialists, and the social justice groups are all part of the same murderous ideology. And don't think just of the usual suspects like Russia and China. Argentina under Peròn ruined its economy by socialism and ended up with 1,200 percent inflation, and Chile under what's his name, Allende, in the seventies with 476 percent inflation. Just look at Venezuela—the new socialist killing has already begun. In Venezuela, you are not allowed to put starvation on the certificate as a cause of death of a child. Or Australia, where the Greens, in the pretense of saving the planet, have forced the energy prices up so high that the elderly on fixed incomes can't afford heating or air-conditioning. So another extinction is on the way, this time of the elderly, with heat stroke, freezing, and starvation."

"You're kidding, Max, in Australia?"

"The country which exports most of the world's uranium does not have a single nuclear reactor. The country that exports coal to the rest of the world has dynamited its own coal-fired electricity plants. They now have electricity shortages. They are not alone. Scotland sits on a sea of oil but refuses to drill."

"Are these people crazy?"

"In a sense, yes. This is not rational. It is a new form of religion. It allows them to ignore reality, and it will only get worse."

"Do you think that this insanity will come here to the US?"

"It is here already. They came in the 1930s. America took them in when they fled from their socialist brothers in Nazi Germany. The National Socialists wanted to kill the International Socialists, but they were both socialists. One would have thought that they might have shown a bit of gratitude, but not them! A man called Adorno and his fellow socialist travelers, who were also rescued by the Americans from Nazi Germany, set out to destroy America. They called themselves the Frankfurt School, and within seventy years, they had succeeded. They reduced the US universities' arts and humanities faculties to a smoking ruin stuffed full of people who knew nothing and taught nothing except internally incoherent, destructive, murderous ideologies."

"It is surely not that bad."

"It is really bad. So-called identity politics or multiculturalism is a product of postmodernism. You are simply part of a group, and the group rules. You are allowed no individual capacity to think or feel. If you believe in this, then you are trapped forever in your own tiny ghetto. In universities, they talk about diversity. But they don't understand that there is more diversity within a group than across groups. It is really antidiversity and insults those who feel that they are individuals and who express any competency in anything."

"Surely that is only a small group?"

"Yes, but it starts in the academe and spreads, especially via human resources departments. It now covers multiple fields within a university, including all fields called studies. Now kids can graduate with a degree in literature who have never read any Shakespeare. They don't even know the names of Milton and Kit Marlowe."

"Milton I know a little, but Marlowe?"

"Ah! You are changing the subject, Sheila. Of course you do.

> Was this the face that launched a thousand ships?
> And dashed the topless towers of Ilium?"

"Well, yes, I have heard of that, but I thought you would cheer me up. Instead you are making me more depressed with your revelations."

"Revelations, yes! I should reread that book in the Bible, Revelations. It looks like St. John was correct. Previously, I thought he was just insane. Now I am not so sure."

"Stop it, Max. I don't like being the fourth horseman of the Apocalypse, the woman on the pale horse. I would rather be someone happy."

"Go find your lover, Sheila.

> Happy, happy happy pair
> None but the brave
> None but the brave
> Deserve the fair."

"I wish."

"Sheila, you are in limbo. Find a way out.

>   Side beside because our fate damned us ere our birth,
>   We stole out of Limbo Gate looking for the Earth.
>   Hand in pulling hand amid fears no dreams had known
>   Sheila ran with me she did, Sheila all alone.

"Go hunting, *ma pauvre*."

"Someday, Max. Maybe someday I will be brave enough. Good night, sleep well."

Chapter 16

John's Journey

Who am I? What do I want to do? Is this all there is? Where do I go from here?

John sat up in his hospital bed. His mind was clear, or he thought it was clear. He remembered more or less his admission through the emergency department the evening before. What he did remember with excruciating clarity was the poorly concealed scorn of the female internal medicine resident who had to interview, examine, and admit him. She had known that he was a doctor.

"I don't know why I am wasting my time with this," she muttered with ill-concealed resentment as she did a paracentesis—removed a couple of liters of fluid from his bloated belly.

He knew that there was more free fluid, but she had no interest in taking any more out. After an interminable wait, he was taken to a room where he fell asleep. Interestingly, there were no nightmares and no DTs. There were not really any shakes when he woke up in the morning. He felt lethargic but not unwell. He even wondered about discharging himself, but after looking at his swollen legs, he eventually decided that he should stay until the lab work was back so that he could see what damage he had done to his body with alcohol.

There would be ultrasounds to assess his liver and kidneys and a few other investigations as he knew that his chest X-ray had shown fluid in his lung bases. Obviously, he had multisystem failures, and unless he stopped drinking alcohol, he would not be long for this world. Maybe it was already too late.

Strangely, he felt no need for alcohol. For several months now, that would have been his first thought on awakening, something he would have had to fight against, the thought of a morning drink, which he could not have if he was working that day. He would have to fight against that desire the whole day at work, watching the clock. When his shift at the walk-in clinic was ending, he would empty one of these easily concealable airline bottles of vodka before going home and then have his first real drink of the day. A couple of big drinks and he could then settle down into a gentle haze with no responsibilities, no worries, no concerns, no regrets, no past, no future—a sort of quasi Nirvana.

> Far and forgot to me is near,
> Shadow and sunlight are the same,
> The vanished gods to me appear
> And one to me is shame and fame.

With nothing to look at except the bare walls of his hospital room, he considered his life. He knew the road he had followed to get there but had always fought shy of analyzing it with any depth. He had never felt much need to do so.

There had been nothing exceptional about his childhood, nothing terribly good and nothing terribly bad. As an excellent student, he had his pick of possible choices at university. His father, mindful of the parlous state of the UK both economically and socially, had suggested medicine as even if nothing else functioned, all elected governments would support the British National Health Service no matter how bad or inept it was. The populace believed, as the media told them endlessly, that it was the wonder of the world, so he would always have some sort of a job.

He had gone into medicine because he neither particularly liked nor disliked it. He had wanted to study literature, but his father had pointed out that a degree in that field qualified him to teach only. If he wanted, he could become a university professor, a reasonably high-status job but poorly paid and, in his father's estimation, a total waste of his talents. His father pointed out that he could learn all the literature he wanted on his own time. There was no need to listen to the opinions of some barely literate professor.

His family was not wealthy, so to supplement his government scholarship, he worked on a relative's farm during breaks from school and university. Looking back, the work did not seem to be as bad as it seemed at the time. Years later, in a bar in London, he compared terrible jobs with a Southern Italian girl he had met. She told him that the worst job she had had was picking almonds up a tree with bugs dropping on her hair.

He told her that his worst job was making silage, food for the cattle to eat over winter. This was fresh cut green grass stored in a tall silo. He would be up inside the silo on the pile of grass with more coming up the auger, which he had to spread about to even the pile out. A layer of molasses would then be sprinkled on the grass and then more grass on top. As the molasses would inevitably splash on them, the boys who did that job were stripped to the waist. When the molasses got on them, the bugs from the green grass would stick to them. He had laughed and joked with the girl over other awful jobs they had had. She mentioned mosquitoes, and he told her of horse flies, the big black silent marauder. You only knew it was there when it bit, and the bite was as if your arm was being torn off, or so it had felt like at the time.

He told that girl also how dangerous a farm could be. Having worked on one herself, she already knew how easy it was to lose a finger here and there. He described what had happened on a farm beside the one where he was working. He had been in the next field just over the fence, so he saw it unfold. A farmer was savaged by his own bull. John could never decide if the experience was horrifying or just another life experience. The farmer had gone into the field with his bull, which, without any warning, had attacked him, knocked him down, and was trying to gore him. The farmer was trying desperately to get away. His shouts attracted the attention of the workers, who ran over. John then witnessed the bravest thing he ever saw in his whole life.

The farmer's middle-aged wife climbed the gate into the field and, armed only with a dish towel she had been using, ran at the bull, who by now was on top of her husband. The men were afraid to go near the maddened animal. She struck it in the face with her dish towel and managed to distract it enough that the men dared to go in and drag her husband out of the field. They flagged down the local minister who happened to be driving by and got the grievously injured man into his car. The farmer died on the way to the hospital.

At university, John had no particular problems with his studies. He quite liked the idea of surgery, so helped in the operating room when he got a chance. He did not find the coursework particularly difficult. There was the usual student's drinking and fooling around, but as a scholarship boy, he had to pass his examinations otherwise the scholarship would have gone away. He was shy and awkward, so his contact with girls tended to be a quick fumble, and after the first time or two, they would lose interest in each other.

In the student's union one day, he looked up and saw something different. She was an incredibly pale-skinned, green-eyed redhead. He thought she was the most glorious thing he had ever seen in his life. He managed to overcome his shyness, got out of his chair, and spoke to her. To his amazement, she smiled at him and was quite friendly. They talked. He found she was in an arts program, was a few years older than he, and planned on doing a PhD in English literature.

They became instantaneous friends and, soon, lovers. Her home was in London, so he was not with her during the summer vacation as he had to work on the farm. When classes began in the fall, unwilling to face such a prolonged absence again, he proposed marriage. She agreed, so they did and moved in together. During their remaining time at university, they were very happy, perhaps not blissful but as near to bliss as John could imagine with very few fights and very few disagreements. He was finishing his final year in medical school when one of the consultants he was assisting in the operating room that day suggested he emigrate.

The consultant had just had a research grant proposal turned down by the central authorities and was very unhappy. He knew that John wanted to be a surgeon.

"Boy," he said, "there is no future in this country. It is old and tired and has lost its way. America is the world's last best hope. Go do your surgical training there. Apply to my old friend George D'Onofrio, the professor of surgery in Miami, and use my name."

Until then, John had never really thought seriously about leaving the UK. He asked the other consultant surgeons for their advice. To his amazement, they all said to go. Not a single one suggested he stay. Some said go to Australia, but most to America. One said that years ago, he would have suggested Canada, but the regulations for that country had changed, and it was now very difficult for European-trained doctors to emigrate there.

Stunned, John talked things over with his wife. She had never considered emigration either, but on reflection, she could see no particular reason to stay. She thought that with her newly awarded PhD, it might be easier to get an academic job in the US than in the UK.

John applied and, in due course, received acceptance into the surgical residency program in Miami, and after the usual bureaucratic problems, the pair eventually arrived in the US. With the help of John's Miami professor, his wife obtained a job in the university arts department. It did not pay very well, but there were benefits and health-care coverage. John liked his new job. The hours were long of course, although his professor told him not as long as they had been years before when he had been a resident. He was keen and always available to take on extra duties as required and so became well-liked.

John and Mary, his wife, grew to love Miami with the sun and the vibrant culture. Very quickly they learned to speak a little Spanish, enough to get by. They looked forward to becoming American citizens as soon as possible. Their lives were calm and placid, and they made no particular plans for the future. When John finished his surgical residency, there would be time enough to decide where to go and what to do.

In his second year of residency, while John was working in an outpatient clinic, he got a phone call. He picked it up but could hardly recognize the voice. It was his wife, Mary, but she was hysterical and so distraught he really couldn't understand what she was saying or what the problem was. After a few minutes, she calmed down enough to tell him that she had a breast lump aspirated by her doctor a month before, and she had just received word that it was cancer. The report had been misfiled in the doctor's office, and he had only just found it and called her. John had known about the aspiration but, as no news is good news, had forgotten about it.

There was no way he could leave the clinic immediately, and there was nothing that could be done immediately in any case. It was a couple of hours before he was able to find a replacement to cover for him, and then he hurried home. He found her agitated and distraught. He tried to embrace her, but she pulled away. It was almost as if she was blaming him that the report had been misfiled in her doctor's office. Eventually she calmed down but was extremely unhappy when he pointed out that they could not make any plans until they had further information and a more accurate diagnosis.

The next month was very difficult. It turned out that she was carrying the BRCA mutation gene that made her liable to develop breast and ovarian cancer. The tumor had spread to a proximal lymph node. Mary spent hours studying the internet and eventually decided to have a bilateral mastectomy and have both ovaries removed at the same sitting.

John was aghast as he had looked forward to having children eventually. But, as he told himself, he was a man of honor, and he had said the words "in sickness and in health till death do us part." He was not happy, but she was his wife, and he would go along with her decision.

Surgery was carried out. Mary had wanted an immediate breast reconstruction with implants. Things went wrong. There was a collection of fluid and wound breakdown, and a few weeks later, one of the implants had to be removed. That was followed by weeks of daily dressing changes. The radiation and the chemo made her very ill. Several months later, another implant was inserted, but then it began to leak. Another surgery to replace it was carried out.

By this time, Mary was gun-shy and completely paranoid. They were saline-filled implants as lawsuits had driven cosmetically superior silicone implants off the market, so they could ripple. Every little ripple or bulge anywhere drove her into paroxysms of terror. Mary felt unable to work, so she remained at home with nothing to do except study the internet endlessly for information on breast cancer. The constant worry led her to develop panic attacks.

Every night when John came home from work, there was a litany of new physical complaints and terrors. There were repeated CT scans and MRIs and any other new experimental scan developed anywhere in the US. In her distress, she began to develop headaches and dizziness leading to a fresh round of brain scans and visits to neurologists and neurosurgeons with more scans.

While she knew, or perhaps understood intellectually, that she was likely having panic attacks, the overwhelming sense of having a heart attack and doom forced her to call repeatedly for an ambulance, and she and John spent many nights in emergency rooms while duplicate tests were repeated, all predictably negative. But as the emergency room doctors told him, given the complaints, what else could they do? If there were anything wrong and they had not done the tests, they would have been sued for negligence.

Then there was the food. When the nausea of the chemo passed off, there was the vegan phase because that was what she had seen on YouTube. When she was too nauseated, he would cook; but when she got a little better, it was the most recent superfood from the internet. She fell for the whole gamut—broccoli, avocado, whatever, and kale. John told her one of the reasons he left Scotland was that his mother cooked kale. He did not want a knockdown, drag-'em-out fight over food given her emotionally fragile state, so he got into the habit of having a burger or a pizza and a couple of drinks on the way home from work so he would not have to eat much of what she called food.

Throughout all this, John tried to remain calm. He liked to tell himself that this was a phase and would eventually pass like a bad dream, that they would be together again as lovers, man and wife. But it never did. It seemed endless. Months became years. The complaints seemed to be getting more fantastical, not less. It was very difficult to come home in the evening after listening to people complain all day about real physical problems to then having to listen to complaints that were clearly not physical. Even if Mary knew somewhere in her brain that her complaints made no sense, that did not make them any less real to her or her voicing them any less vociferous.

Sitting listening to this litany of woes, real or otherwise, for an hour or more every day starting the moment he came in the front door, was extraordinarily wearing. He would pour himself a very stiff vodka tonic before he sat down to listen. He found he had to listen in silence as any advice he offered was immediately and scornfully rejected. Soon he switched to a larger glass, which became mostly vodka with very little tonic. By this time, Mary had given up drinking alcohol completely. One drink became two, and he noticed her looking disapprovingly at his drink, so he cut down on the size by surreptitiously having a very large drink straight out of the bottle before he came to join her to listen to the complaints of that day. The pleasant buzz of the alcohol made the listening tolerable. He felt unable to express his own distress and loneliness in the face of this unending wail of misery and fear. He found it impossible to ask for love or even touch, some human contact.

One day, she opened a cupboard she seldom used and saw three 40 oz bottles of vodka sitting there. She looked at him with disapproval and shook her head. Thereafter, he began to hide the bottles. After the first few times when she called an ambulance knowing what to expect, he would have a big drink straight from the bottle before they left the house and put a Mickey in his pocket to drink in the washrooms in the emergency department while they waited patiently for the tests to be completed.

He would go to bed early as really there was nothing to say to Mary as in silence she endlessly searched the internet for the latest news on breast cancer. This meant that no matter how much he drank, he was always fit for work the next day. When he voiced his difficulties to others, they told him of men leaving their wives during a crisis like that as they were simply unable to cope with the stress and the endless litany of complaints. John prided himself that he was a man, that he was a rock, utterly dependable. His own distress made him much more sympathetic to and understanding of patients in the same situation, and patients vocally appreciated this deep and unexpected understanding.

The chemo fog, his colleagues warned him, would affect her thinking and last for about a couple of years. He was hopeful that things were improving, but then things got bad again, and there was more trouble with the breast implants. Real or imaginary, John never knew. Mary elected to have both removed permanently. During this whole time, there had been no sex. Mary had not felt that she wanted it, and John did not know how to ask in the face of this alternate suffering or indifference.

Mary's fear gradually receded, and the panic attacks and the visits to the emergency departments slowly decreased, but there was no increase in tenderness. She really did not want to be touched. She was uncomfortable being hugged, and a kiss was a chaste peck on the lips. A hand on her thigh or shoulder was simply allowed to lie there, or she would actively move away.

Surely she will get over this sometime, thought John, or in moments of despair, *Is this what it is going to be forever?*

Mary never did return to work. Initially, she felt too ill and then too foggy. But even after a couple of years, she showed no interest at all in returning to employment. John did not want to push her. It was financially very tight trying to live on a surgical resident's salary, but with a fair amount of borrowing, he managed it by spending almost nothing on himself other than the vodka, which was the only thing that kept him sane.

He would have a few drinks, go for a walk on his own, read some poetry and stories of the long past, and go to bed early. With the vodka, he had begun to snore at night, so she did not want to sleep beside him. As there was no togetherness and no tenderness, he did not object, accepting that that simply was another cross to bear. She was after all probably correct. He probably did snore in his drunken state. But it was a slow death. He thought of Shakespeare, whom he found much more comforting to read than anything modern.

> Tomorrow and tomorrow and tomorrow
> creeps on this petty pace,
> From one day until the end of time.

This will be all my tomorrows, he thought in despair. *I have to leave. I have to get out.* But then he thought, *I can't leave. I made a vow to look after her—not that she wants looking after. She does not seem to want any contact with me at all.* They hardly spoke. He would eat some junk food before he came home, drink, read a little, mostly poetry of a bygone era, and go to bed early while she silently watched movies on her computer or searched YouTube for additional information about breast cancer.

Most of the time, he was numb and tried not to think about it. When he did, the sense of loss and longing was overwhelming. *Is this all there is to it? This is going to be it for the rest of my life.* He remembered a story, or was it a poem, by Kipling.

> As she lay by my side,
> Day by day and night by night
> I grew to hate her.
> Would to God that she or I had died.

He finished his residency and found positions at local hospitals as he was actually a technically excellent and well-liked surgeon, and his reputation steadily grew. He spent all his time working as there was nothing for him at home. He preferred sixteen-hour workdays where he was with people who liked him, appreciated him, and would talk to him; so he rapidly paid off the debts he had incurred. Work till you drop, have a few drinks, and go to bed drunk and exhausted—rinse and repeat endlessly, a life with no meaning, no beginning, and no end.

His wife aged in front of him. Clearly, she was not taking the hormone replacement prescribed as a consequence of the removal of her ovaries. He could hardly believe she was only in her early thirties. Eventually, she made the decision to go home. Her parents were still alive, living in the outskirts of London. She felt that there was nothing to keep her in the US.

One morning, as he was on his way out the door, when uncharacteristically she was awake and up and about, she told him she was leaving. There had been no warning. She said she had a plane booked for that afternoon and would not be back. All she wanted was $2 million, either up-front or in installments. If he gave her that, she would not ask for more and would give him a divorce. He agreed immediately, feeling empty, nothing, wished her luck, and without any physical contact, left for work. He could not think of anything else to say.

When he returned to an empty house that evening, he got a bottle of vodka out from its hiding place, sat down with his feet up on the coffee table, and had a long drink. He did not know how he felt. A sense of sorrow? A sense of relief? Freedom? Get another woman? Not likely, one had been quite enough. He had had almost no sex for six years other than the odd prostitute. He had run out of desire. And yet, and yet, there was sorrow that brought tears to his eyes. He had failed. They had failed. Their vows had failed. All their hopes and all their dreams 'in the glad morning of our days' dust and ashes. Ah Christ! It had been hell for the last few years, and yet he felt overwhelmed with grief. 'Have all thy glories, triumphs, spoils, shrunk to this little measure?' It was like a death.

> All my life's bliss from thy dear life was given
> All my life's bliss is in the grave with thee.

What the hell was he doing anyway? He could pay her off soon, then it would be all over. "Stay in Miami? Spend the rest of my life doing Mickey Mouse gallbladder surgery? Screw it all. I need a new place and a new job and a new life. Maybe the military for a complete change."

Sitting in the hospital bed that morning after his latest drunk, he realized that this was the end of that journey—the hell of Afghanistan, Sheila, his unexpected lover, his bright star, then one more disaster: tossed out of the army, the long drunk. "Even the medical resident thinks I am a total screw-up, a moron not worth wasting her time on. I have truly hit bottom. I have got to get myself together. I have to stop feeling sorry for myself. Man up! Pull your goddamn socks up! Put a plug in the jug. Time to dry out and go to AA."

Chapter 17

The Quest

Sheila eventually took her courage in both hands, and one afternoon when she woke up, she emailed the clinic where she thought John was working as a consultant. She checked her email before she left for work that evening. There was a reply. It read, "Sheila. Is that really you? I am so glad you reached out. Could we meet?" And he left her his telephone number.

She looked at it for a while, and then with her heart in her mouth she called him. He picked up. "Hello."

She recognized his voice. "John."

"Sheila! Sheila, is that you? Oh, thank God I have found you. When I recovered, I did not know where to begin to look. You vanished after you left the military."

"Are you well?"

"Yes. Dry now for over a year, and you?"

"No drugs, no booze for nine months now. I have a job in a nursing home here in Detroit."

"I work at a walk-in clinic in Chicago. I would really love to see you."

"Of course. I have next weekend off. Where should we meet?"

"My accommodation is not that great."

"Neither is mine. Maybe New Orleans."

"I would love to, but the temptation might be just too great. Better to be in a place we can maybe attend an AA meeting with some people one of us knows."

"Yes, of course you are right. 'Remember When!' I'll come to Chicago. Let me book a flight, and I'll get back to you. I am working night shift, and my shift finishes at 7:00 a.m. on Saturday morning, so I will try to be there sometime around noon."

Late Saturday morning, they met at O'Hare Airport. When she had last seen him, he was bloated and unkempt. Now he was as she remembered him in Afghanistan, slim and clean. He was neatly dressed in slacks, polished loafers, and a sports jacket, actually wearing a collar and tie. She recognized him immediately as she came out of baggage claim. She was by now accustomed to passing people doing a hastily concealed double take when they saw her scarred face.

He saw her and opened his arms, she flew to him, embracing him.

"John. John, I have missed you so."

"Sheila. God, it is good to see you."

They held the embrace for a long minute, and then still holding him tight, she kissed him.

"Let's get the El and go downtown."

They had a late lunch, then spent the day wandering in wonder, holding onto each other and stealing glances as if afraid that they would get lost again. There was no burning desire for sex, just a longing for contact, for touch, and for forgiveness. They walked the streets and then walked along the lakeshore. After an early dinner, they went to his AA home group meeting where she introduced herself as an out-of-town visitor.

That night, they made love tentatively and tenderly as if afraid that something would break. Both were unused to it as Sheila had not had sex or even felt like it since her dry date, when she had her last drink of alcohol. Before that, she remembered the wildness and the craziness and was ashamed of what she had been and what she had done.

John tried to apologize again that he had not somehow gotten her out of Afghanistan before that terrible event that had ruined her life. She told him it was not his fault, it was hers. She had ignored medical advice and had wanted to stay with him. They held hands as they shared their sadness and guilt.

She felt overcome with remorse at her moment of insanity that fateful night when she was unable to contain her anger. But she also bubbled over with bitterness at those who had placed young people in that impossible position where they were expected to listen to children being tortured and raped by their so-called allies. They both felt a sense of betrayal that they had been asked to build a nation where none had ever existed and likely none ever would—a culture probably destined to remain in the Dark Ages with no hope of improvement where women were forced to cover themselves with black bags and assaulted and killed when they tried to get any education and where little boys were fair game for rape.

"Bomb them if they shelter terrorists, but that only makes the rubble dance around," said John. "No one seems interested in actually following the money where it all comes from to fund these terrorists. And yet everyone knows. That's the tragedy, or the farce. Everybody knows, and yet nothing gets done. Certainly no boots on the ground ever. Our guys are still in that shithole, accomplishing what exactly? The Taliban are back in force aided by the Pakistan Military Intelligence, a fact which everyone knows and no one does anything about. They pretend it is not happening."

"The world is mad. You and I, we are just the wastage along the way, the flotsam and jetsam."

"Ah, screw them all. Fuck Washington. I have found you again, Sheila."

"But my face. The only place I would be comfortable is the masked ball either in Rio or Venice."

"Maybe someday we will go there. But, Sheila, that is a very small part of you. I don't see it. I read a book once whose name I can't remember. It must have been in the 1800s in the north of England. It was about a traveling weaver. He was passing through a village. There was a girl with a harelip. The villagers, egged on by one guy, probably a guy who wanted her body, were going to do something to her. Maybe they thought she was a witch. 'Hare shotton,' they called her face. The weaver saves her. It must have been Cumberland because he challenges the leader to wrestle. 'Oot wrostle,' he says. He wins and takes the girl with him."

"So love conquers all?"

"Sing for faith and hope are high / None so true as you and I / Sing the lovers litany / Love like ours can never die.

"Sheila, never leave me. Be with me forever."

"Until the stars fall, John."

Chapter 18

The Great Betrayal

"How are you, Max? You are looking well." John was visiting him while he was in the hospital where he had been taken after suffering a stroke. Fortunately, it seemed to be a mild one. His doctors were optimistic about his recovery.

"Not bad. I can speak. No paralysis, no problems. Just fuzzy in the head and not quite certain of myself. Where is Sheila?"

"She was here to see you yesterday and said you were doing well. She is off today with some friends having a ladies luncheon."

"Oh yes, and how many ladies?"

"I don't know. Just some friends."

"She will be seeing her lover and his friends and have a good time with all three lovers at once."

"What are you talking about?"

"John, John, Sheila likes lovers—all shapes and sizes and as many as she can get at once—ever since she was a child. She told me a week ago she had fun that afternoon with two men at once."

"What are you saying? You crazy? You're delusional!"

"I am as sane as you are. It is just that I have decided to tell the truth. No more cover-up. Sheila fucks like a rabbit. Always did, always will. The other night she got Hal the orderly to come and fuck her in front of me. She may have a scarred face, but her legs and tits are very nice. She likes to show them to me."

"She does?"

"Oh yes. Sometimes she has me stroke her."

"You never mentioned this before. You never said anything."

"I never felt any reason to. Now I that I have felt death up close and personal, I am thinking I should change and tell other people the truth. I feel sorry for you."

John was stunned. Max had known Sheila for over a year now. She, by her own admission, spent some time almost every night with Max. All of a sudden, his life fell apart. All his desperate insecurities came flooding back. The insecurities he had had since he was a child suddenly overwhelmed him. He turned and left the room, bumping into the door on the way out. He could not speak. He felt light-headed. He could not think.

The darkness returned—the misery of the life he had lived with his first wife, the awfulness of Afghanistan, the suicide bomber, the filth and the misery of the Kandahar hospital, the horror of these young GIs with their genitals blown off, Sheila's tragic collapse, his alcoholic breakdown, his redemption. Redemption! He had been living a lie for the last few months, a fantasy. He had known that when she was younger, she had slept around. She had been doing that when he first met her in Afghanistan. She had told him that after her discharge from Brook, the hospital in San Antonio, and the army, she had been wild, in the grip of full-blown alcoholism, doing crazy things; but she had told him that after her dry date, when she stopped drinking, there had been no man but him. He had moved to Detroit to be with her and had obtained a job there, and they had been living together. And now it seemed all she had told him was a lie.

He was speechless. Stunned, he left the hospital and walked the streets. His mind was in a whirl. He had been living a lie. He had been betrayed. He could have understood it if they had both still been drunks. Drunks make promises, and no one believes them. But this! The AA meetings they had attended together. The undying love they had sworn. The dreams they had of children, which they had found was not possible. Her gynecologist said she had internal scarring, possibly from infections. At that information, he had been disappointed but philosophical. Now he was enraged. *Multiple infections*, he thought. *What a whore!*

He had looked over the edge of the abyss and had painfully struggled back to sanity and respectability. He had dreamed of the future they would have together. All a lie! He walked past a bar.

"Fuck it all. Stay sober for what? Another kick in the teeth, another betrayal?" He went in and up to the bar. "Give me a cold one," he said, pointing to the beer tap, "and a double shot of rye."

"Having a hard day?" asked the man sitting at the bar beside him nursing a beer.

"You don't know the half of it," John said, downing the rye in two swallows. He felt it burn all the way down and almost immediately got the dopamine hit. The room brightened, and he felt immeasurably better. Everything will be just fine. He did not need anyone. He could cope with anything—lies, betrayal by that scarred slut. *Why stay in this dump of a town with this lousy climate? Go south. Get a job in Miami. The sun and the sea. No reason to stay here.*

He had another double rye. He felt his mind clear, and what he should do was obvious. *Leave now*, he thought. *Get on a plane.* He took a cab back to their apartment, threw his few belongings into his roller bag, called an Uber, and left for the airport. The alcoholic buzz was high and powerful. *Easy come, easy go*, he thought.

At the airport, he noticed a flight to Tampa leaving shortly. He bought a ticket, lined up for security, and left. On the plane, he had a couple of drinks. He had switched off his phone when he left the hospital. Sheila had been seeing Max almost every night since she had worked in that place. He had been her companion and confessor. *If only they had told me earlier*, he thought. *Ah well, too bad.*

On arrival in Tampa, he checked into a cheap motel and found a liquor store nearby. He bought two 40-oz bottles of vodka. Back at his room, he locked the door, opened a bottle, and took a long slug. He felt better. He sat down to think. *There is nothing for me in this world. It has all turned into shit. Everything has gone wrong, and everyone I trusted has betrayed me. What is the point in going on? Drink this lot and never waken up. That slut deceived me and lied to me. She betrayed me. I suffer and she gets away with it. Well, fuck that, and fuck her. She might as well have a hard time too. These nurses are always killing their patients in these nursing homes. An accusation will make her lose her job. She might as well feel as bad as I do. Serves her right.*

He found the retirement home administrator's number on his cell phone. He wanted to remain anonymous, so to be certain, he went outside and found a pay phone. The call went to an answering machine. "Sheila Lillehammer has been killing you residents with insulin," he said and hung up the phone. He went back to his room; made sure his own phone was switched off, and picked up the bottle.

The next day, when the maid came to clean his room, she knocked on the door. There was no answer. She came back a few hours later. There was still no answer, so she got the motel manager. When they opened the door, they found John passed out on the bed. They immediately called an ambulance, and he was taken to the nearest hospital emergency department, still unconscious.

It was twenty-four hours later that he woke up, unable to remember what had happened. Over the next few hours, his mind cleared. The motel people had packed his belongings into his bag and sent it with him, but his phone was missing. The bitterness of his betrayal came back. He was listless and depressed. By that time, the hospital personnel felt he was fit for discharge. Where he went from there was his problem, not theirs.

Fuck it, he thought and went off to get another drink. Two days later, he was walking down the street. It was late morning, so he was relatively sober. He had lost his possessions but, amazingly, still had his wallet. As he was passing a newspaper stand, he saw Sheila's face on the cover of the newspaper. In bold letters, it said, "Nurse Accused of Killing Patients."

What? He thought, confused. Then he remembered. *That telephone call. Oh Jesus, no! It was not serious! It was meant to get her into trouble. Revenge only, not criminal. There must be a mistake. I gotta get back to Detroit and clear this up.*

He got a cab to the airport. Fortunately, no one had stolen his wallet. All thoughts of alcohol were gone. He cleaned himself up in the airport washrooms as best as possible and got the next flight back to Detroit. He was tortured with the thought of how corrupt the US justice system was. If some DA was looking for a political appointment, she would be convicted, guilty or innocent. Suppose she had done it? It was not as uncommon as most people thought. Patients whose life had become a painful burden asked all the time for help into the next world. It was easy enough to slip the occasional patient a few extra sleeping pills.

John had never worked in a palliative care unit, but he remembered as an intern in the UK, many years before, ordering increasing doses of morphine for those who were suffering painfully from terminal cancer. Everyone knew that if enough were given, the patient would go to sleep permanently. But there was never any official policy, and John was not aware of any official policy in any country. In a palliative care unit, there were never accusations of wrongful death. In those units, all people were ever asking for was a relatively painless demise. But this was not a palliative unit; this was a retirement home, a nursing home. If convicted, she would get life in prison, or even—did they have the death penalty in New York State?

? He did not think so but did not know.

He took a cab from the airport to the central police station. No one wanted to speak to him. He persisted, and eventually, hours later, as he refused to leave, the detective involved in the case agreed to see him. John had always been told to never talk to the police about anything without a lawyer being present. But he had lost his phone and not yet bought a new one, and she was innocent.

He saw the detective in the interrogation room with the recorder on. He gave his particulars and how he knew Sheila. He told them that they had had a lover's spat, and in a moment of anger, he had left that message on the administrator's telephone answering machine. Sheila was completely innocent. There had never been any suggestion of her killing anyone.

"Never killed anyone?" said the detective. "How about the trouble in Afghanistan? I heard from my sources there was a killing there."

John was stunned. "But it was an accident. They were raping a child!"

"It is true then. She did kill someone and got off."

John realized his mistake. He should never have talked to the police. He had only made things infinitely worse for her. He needed a lawyer. He immediately stopped talking.

"I have nothing more to say. I want a lawyer," he said.

The detective pressured him, but John remained silent. Eventually the detective gave up. "Then you had better get a lawyer and come back. We will have to talk again later. You cannot go back to her apartment. That is still a crime scene."

They would not let him talk to her. John left the police station and grabbed a cab to take him to the nursing home. By the time he got there, the night shift was on duty. He found one of the PSWs who had been close to Sheila. This was the woman who had courageously tackled Crazy Bob when he was attacking Max. He asked her how Max was.

"I don't know. Since he came back from the hospital, he has not been making sense. He is accusing me of displaying myself in front of him and bringing a lover into his room and having sex in front of him when we thought he was asleep. He is crazy. I am a married woman. There is something wrong with him. He also accused Sheila of bringing men into his room at night and having sex with them. That is nonsense. There are no men here at night, except the orderly, and he is gay. Then there is this nonsense about Sheila being accused of killing people. That is also crazy. I was here most nights. Sheila would either be making rounds, helping us, or talking to Max. We knew always where she was all the time. These charges are wrong."

John felt the bottom fall out of his stomach. *Nonsense! Max had been talking nonsense. Sheila had never been unfaithful.*

He went into the room. Max was sitting in his chair. He had taken his clothes off.

"Ah John. Did you bring Sheila for a little sex?"

"Hush now, Max," said the PSW who had accompanied him. "Don't say silly things like that."

"Don't you want to have sex with me again?"

The PSW laughed at him. "In your dreams. Now, Max, get your clothes back on."

John left the room. Max was clearly confused. *What have I done? Did Sheila really kill some of them? Sweet Jesus Christ. What do I do now?*

Chapter 19

The Inquisition

"Come on, miss, hands behind your back."

The handcuffs clicked on. Sheila felt despair. Why would they need to handcuff her? Was it deliberately done to produce a feeling of helplessness and guilt? They escorted her down the elevator and into the back seat of a police patrol car. A hand was placed on the top of her head, pushing her down as she entered the car. Again, to produce a feeling of helplessness? At the police station, the paperwork was done, and she was shown into a bare room where there was a table and two chairs. One of them was occupied by a balding overweight middle-aged man. A grim-faced woman stood in the corner, leaning against a wall. Her handcuffs were removed, and she was asked to be seated. The seated man clicked on a tape recorder and announced the names of those present.

"Well, Miss Lillehammer, we have evidence that you killed a dozen people in your nursing home. How many did you kill in the other nursing homes you worked?"

"None. I killed no one."

"You mean none at the other nursing homes?"

"No. I mean none."

"Come on now. We have been told you did. We know you did. You injected them with insulin."

"Just the ones who were diabetic."

"So you admit you killed the diabetics?"

"No, no. I did not say that."

"Yes, you did. You just said you did."

Sheila realized she was making a mistake. She had to stop talking. They were twisting everything she said. She had seen interviewers do just that on television. "So what you are saying is …"

"No, I never said that."

She had seen these hostile 'gotcha' interviews again and again. She knew enough from watching TV to refuse to answer any further questions.

"I want a lawyer."

"After we have talked to you and after you have admitted that you killed all these people."

"I never did. I thought that there was a presumption of innocence."

The detective laughed. "What century did you grow up in?"

Sheila closed her lips and, in spite of a barrage of questions and browbeating, refused to say anything. The next day, a public defender showed up. He wanted her to sign documents; she refused as she did not trust him. He had a briefcase full of files and papers, and he was in a hurry.

"You have been accused of multiple murders," he said. "Let me plea bargain for you. You are going to go to jail. The only question is, how long? This DA, we call him Torquemada, the leader of the Spanish inquisition, wants to run for mayor, so he needs convictions of noncolored middle-class people."

Sheila was appalled. She refused to give this man any signatures. She was lost. She could not contact John. Max had been irrational when she saw him. Nothing he said made sense. Obviously, the stroke was much worse than they had feared. He was in no position to help her. She sat in jail. She could not believe this was legal—perhaps in some South American banana republic or the Middle East, but not in the US.

On day 3, she was taken to an interview room where a well-dressed, lean, hawk-faced man was waiting for her.

"Ms. Lillehammer, my name is Gary Neinstein. Your friend, Dr. John McCall, has hired me to take your case. If I were you, I would not listen to the public defender you have been provided with. That would not be in your best interest. I need your signature before I can proceed. Dr. McCall has guaranteed payment."

"Where is he? He vanished. Why? I need to speak to him."

"That is currently not possible. Here is the proof of his payment on your behalf."

He passed across some documents and showed her the signature. It was John's. She was amazed at the amount.

"But he does not have that kind of money."

"That is a down payment, and he has promised to pay future costs. My law firm does not do pro bono work."

"Ye gods!"

"Yes, Ms. Lillehammer. You are going to need the gods. The DA will come after you with both guns blazing. He wants to stand for political office, so he needs scalps. And yours would be pretty high profile. Anyway, you need to sign these documents so I can review the charges against you. As I understand it, you are charged with multiple murders at three nursing homes."

"Three?"

"Yes, you worked in three. You clearly don't understand the system. Once knowledge of the charges against you are made public, the lawyers are going to advertise for every family of every patient who died in these nursing homes while you were there and even after you left or maybe who were even just residents there. They are going to come after you in a class action lawsuit. They are not interested in you personally as you have no money; or rather your nurse's insurance is so little it's not worth pursuing. But if you are convicted, they will sue the nursing homes who have real insurance. So you understand there are going to be a lot of witnesses against you. If you are convicted, the witnesses may get some money from the class action. If you go free, they get nothing."

"And this is justice?"

"Don't be naive. This is about money and power. Justice has nothing to do with it. There is potentially a lot of money to be made in this case. So there will be very clever, very hungry lawyers involved. Do not talk to anyone, especially not to your cellmates. You must assume that they are informers, either for the DA or more likely for the class action lawsuit lawyers. Be very careful. Say nothing to anyone."

Later the lawyer sat down with John.

"She is in trouble."

"Why, what evidence have they got?"

"She has admitted to injecting some patients with insulin."

"But they were diabetics, and she is a nurse. That is what nurses do."

"She will be tried in front of a jury who may not know the difference between insulin and Jupiter. The nursing homes have no clear records of how much insulin was used in what cases. All they know is the total quantity brought in. How much has been wasted, as some must have been, they have no idea."

"But surely she said she did not do it?"

"Then they will charge her with perjury because she did give insulin to some patients. And they will charge her with obstruction of justice because she has denied killing anyone."

"But this is a nightmare, like a Kafka story or 1984."

"No, or rather yes. This is the US justice system. It is different. Why do you think you are paying me and not relying on a public defender? The DA really wants to convict her for something. It doesn't matter what as long as he can get publicity."

"So she will go down."

"She will serve time. The question is, for how long?"

"But this can't be happening."

"Look, conviction rates in criminal cases are in excess of 90 percent. Do you really think all who are charged are guilty? In the end, we will have to plea bargain."

John bowed his head and covered his face with his hands in horror and despair. All this was his fault. His fault.

Chapter 20

Oedipus Rex

"Ah, Jane, how are you today?"

"I am well, Max. You sound much better."

"I feel a bit fuzzy in the head. I checked the dates, and I seem to have lost a few days. I am not sure what happened. What did happen?"

"You are getting much better, Max. You don't remember, but you had a stroke about two weeks ago. For a while, you were completely disoriented. You were making no sense. You sound much better now."

"Thank God for that. How is everyone? How is Sheila?"

"Oh, Max. You did not know. Sheila has been arrested and charged with murdering patients."

"What? No! What happened?"

"I don't know. The police came one day and retrieved all the records and questioned the staff. They arrested Sheila the same day, and we have not seen her since."

"Oh *Mon Dieu*! When was that?"

"About ten days ago."

"Where is she?"

"She's in jail. Dr. McCall disappeared for a few days, but he is back and has hired a lawyer to help Sheila."

"He disappeared? Why?"

"No one knows. I am glad you are better, Max. You were saying funny things."

"What things?"

"I really would rather not say. You were confused."

"No! Did I? What did I say about Sheila?"

"Just that she had been running around with other men. You told Dr. McCall. He seemed extremely upset."

"I told John that? *Merde*! I need to speak to him."

"Don't make yourself upset, Max. The doctor says you have to take it easy."

"Please, Jane. Get in contact with Doc John immediately."

"I will try, Max, but I am not sure where he is."

"Administration must have his phone number as Sheila's contact. Could you get it for me please?"

"Yes. They probably do. I will go and ask."

Ten minutes later, she returned smiling and gave him a piece of paper with the telephone number.

"You were right, Max. They did have it."

He phoned immediately, and John picked up.

"John, Max here. I have just recovered from the effects of my stroke. Jane, the PSW, has told me I was saying the most awful things. She told me that I had told you that Sheila was unfaithful."

"Yes, you did, and I believed you. I fell off the wagon, and in my despair, I accused Sheila of overdosing some of the patients, and now she is in jail. The defense lawyer I hired says that she will be convicted."

"Oh God. I am so sorry. I remember nothing before this morning. Jane tells me I was saying the most awful things about Sheila. Dear Christ. She is in jail. What can I do to help?"

"Are you sure your brain's functioning properly now?"

"It seems so, and Jane tells me I am making sense. I still feel a little fuzzy, so over the next few days, my brain will probably recover more. Jane says I told you that Sheila was involved in all sorts of sexual activity, and her too. That was nonsense. Is there anything I can do to help?"

"Start retraining your brain as best you can. And yes, it would help if you have any money I can borrow. These high-priced lawyers are really high priced."

"I have some here and some property in France I can liquidate, but that will take some time."

"I could do with about $50,000 right now. I will be speaking to the lawyer again today, so I will get back to you on exactly how much I will need."

The lawyer had been working for a bail hearing where he was able to convince the judge that she was not a flight risk, but she had to surrender her passport. The judge was dubious and set the bail at $500,000.

Against Sheila's wishes, John contacted her family in Canada. Her father had died and her mother was in a nursing home with early dementia, but he was able to contact one of her four sisters, who contacted the others. John protested her innocence. He promised that if they loaned him the money for the bail bond down payment and provided collateral, he would guarantee to repay the family. Reluctantly, very reluctantly, as they had had no contact with Sheila for years, they put up the money. Sheila was bailed and returned to the apartment they shared. She had to wear an electronic ankle bracelet so the authorities could track her at all times.

John had already faced the agonizing fact that Sheila knew that all this was his fault. He had already told the police and the lawyer that the crank phone call had come from him. He had testified to that at the bail hearing, that it was all a mistake, a lover's spat. Maybe that evidence had helped and maybe not, but the judge had granted bail. He took her home from the jail. They did not know what to say to each other.

She was sickened when she had found out about that fateful phone call. He had betrayed her on the flimsy evidence of a confused poststroke man, and he was a doctor. He was supposed to know these things. How in God's name could he have believed what Max had said about her? Was that what he really thought of her? Was his belief in her really a lie? Was his professed love a lie? Was he just after a quick, clean, convenient fuck? Was that all it was? Was that all it had ever been?

For him, the guilt was crushing. How could he have believed the rambling words of a poststroke patient? He was a doctor for Christ's sake. Where had his brain been when he believed that? He was nothing but a worthless alcoholic, a paranoid idiot who had betrayed the only good person in his miserable life. Make amends? How could he make amends for this colossal—this incomprehensible—blunder? God, how could he have been so angry and so vindictive? Even if she had been unfaithful, she was still the best thing he had ever had. He made repeated attempts to apologize. She could not accept it.

"Just don't, John. Don't. Leave it alone for now. I forgive you."

She knew these were only words. How could she forgive him? She had looked over the edge, right over the edge of the abyss of alcoholism and drugs and had painfully clawed her way back onto solid ground only to be tossed into another bottomless pit.

Pull yourself together, she thought. *You are looking at potentially spending the rest of your life in jail. Maybe I deserve it. I did kill five people, six if you count the Afghan. Maybe that is justice.* She thought of Robert Service's poem and began to weep.

> Was I not born to walk in scorn?
> While other walk in pride.
> The maker marred and evil starred
> I drift upon the tide.

But then she thought of the next lines.

> But he alone shall judge his own
> So I his judgement bide.

John tried to put his arm around her shoulders, but she shrugged him off, still thinking dark thoughts.

Maybe this is God's judgment on me for what I have been, for all my bad decisions. Maybe I should just walk in front of a bus and get it all over with. My life has been mostly misery anyway. Why bother with more of it? God knows I have tried. I stopped the drugs and alcohol. That was not suffering enough. What is the point? Why continue with this miserable existence?

"Tomorrow, and tomorrow and tomorrow creep on this petty pace." One humiliation after another. I am 'on the way to dusty death' anyway. One blast of Fentanyl and all this misery, all this pain is gone. John, John, how could you do this to me? You think you are wracked with guilt? You want me to forgive you for what you have done to me? Just who is the injured party here?

Sure, Max behaved abominably, but he was confused. Of course he had dreams of what he would have liked to do with me and Jane. He is a man who liked women. The stroke merely lifted the inhibitions in his brain for a while and let him express his thoughts and his dreams. Of course! No problem there. But John? He has no excuse. How in the name of God could he possibly have thought I would have lovers in an old age home? Give your damaged, alcohol-burned brain a shake, you fucking moron.

It was therefore a melancholy and silent homecoming to their apartment. He would try to say something, but she would stop it with a raised warning finger. He slept on the sofa that night. She did not want him in bed with her.

The next day, she tried to pull herself together. "The moving finger writes and having writ moves on." "Yesterday is past. It is gone forever." 'One day at a time." "Let go and let God"—all the AA slogans. *God, I need them now. We need to go to an AA meeting. There has to be solace for me somewhere. Is there no hope for the widow's child?*

They found a meeting where they had not previously been. He sat beside her in silent misery. Listening and sharing, she felt some peace descend on her. He suddenly felt her hand on his. He put his arm around her shoulders. He could feel her shuddering in silent weeping. There was nothing to say. They went to another meeting that evening with some people they knew. Most were aware of the charges against her. Some turned away, but most did not believe the charges and welcomed her with handshakes and words of encouragement and a few hugs from some who had faced the prospect of or had been in jail themselves.

That night, after the second meeting, they discussed what to do. They both knew the lawyer's predictions that guilty or innocent, she was looking at jail time.

"We could run away, find ourselves a place up in the northwest, where no one would ever see us."

"Yes, but we would need to work to get some money to live. My face is recognizable. I was saving up for cosmetic surgery, but the funds will all have to go to the lawyer. I would have to remain hidden inside a burka forever. It would be like being in jail."

"Maybe we could escape to Europe. Max says he has a place there."

"Yes, but how? This is not fiction. The storybooks make it sound easy, but I have had to give up my passport. And I don't know how to buy false papers. How do you get a new identity when half of America is looking for a woman with a scarred face? If I get caught, that would be an admission of real guilt, and I would go to jail for life. Besides, paying off the bail bond would cripple my family. I may not like them much, but I could not do that to them."

"Your family was pretty reluctant to help. Maybe we could go to South America, drive across the border into Mexico. That can't be so hard."

"I don't know about that. Have you ever done it? And if we get there, that is a land of constant criminal activity, and if someone recognizes me, we are worse off than ever. There would be blackmail, and I would rather be dead than be a low-class prostitute in one of these countries."

"How about Canada?"

"If we were criminals from Haiti or Somalia that would certainly be a good option. We could claim to be refugees. But we are middle-class Americans. They would immediately send us back."

After discussions with their lawyer, reluctantly, they came to the conclusion that a plea bargain was the only thing that made sense. The lawyer pointed out that it was no secret that the DA would be running for political office. Somehow or other, he would get her convicted of something. He pointed out crime statistics—almost 100 percent conviction rate for something. The DA would not particularly care how much jail time she got, just as long as she got enough to make his conviction rate look good for his campaign. Conviction for something would be enough.

With her permission, her lawyer bargained it down to an assault and battery charge. She pled guilty. The case disappeared from the media, and she was eventually sentenced to two years in jail to be served in a minimum security prison in Florida.

Max remained distraught, blaming himself for the disaster. Money was required to pay the lawyer's fees. Neither he nor John objected to that as in unskilled hands, the outcome could have been infinitely worse. Nonetheless, there were debts to be paid. John was still working as a doctor in the walk-in clinic making reasonable money but not in that league. They discussed the issue.

"I am not sure what to do. I don't think that my pension is transferable after my death. I do have an old fully paid life insurance. If I put it in Sheila's name, the families involved may include her in the ongoing lawsuit against the nursing homes, trying to get more money. So I will have to put it in your name."

"Did she really give insulin to some of these patients, Max?"

"I am sure she did as part of the treatment. We are people here, John, real people sitting around waiting for death, some not so happily. Some of us would like to go sooner than others in spite of what the families now claim. Some of us know we want that and can ask. Others need to but don't know it. There is nothing black-and-white about this. It is not binary, yes or no. There are all gradations, all the messiness of real life with its difficult questions. John, you must support Sheila during her hour of trial. You must wait for her. If you abandon her, I could not bear it. I will have to make sure the insurance money comes your way."

"Make sure of what?"

"My life insurance money. I have lived a long life. Engineering an accident should not be too difficult. This mess is my fault. I suppose I was her Svengali. She put to sleep the first two to protect me and the others because I suggested it."

"You feel no guilt about that?"

"The patients? No, not at all, not one little bit. Sheila helped them out of their suffering in this world into presumably paradise in the next or, at the very least, Nirvana. My guilt is that I confused you. I must check with a lawyer to make sure that my will is up-to-date. If I die within a year, the insurance company may think there is something funny, and maybe my useless families will challenge it. After that time, it should be OK. I will make sure you have a copy of the will."

John thought it was just talk but a copy of Max's will duly arrived naming him as the recipient. He thought nothing of it at the time, just talk. A year later, John, who was now living and working in Miami to be close to Sheila's prison, where he could visit, got a phone call from Max. He had stayed in touch to hear how Sheila was surviving. On this occasion, he was very serious.

"I have talked to the lawyer. He says he sees no significant issue with the will. I am therefore going now, a personal atonement. I hope to see Sheila and you another time and in another place."

"What are you talking about, Max?"

"It is OK, John. You will know. In time, all will be clear. Tell Sheila to read *The Tale of Two Cities*. *Bonsoir et bon chance*, and give my love to Sheila."

He rang off. The next day, the nursing home phoned John as it was his number that Max had left as his next of kin contact.

"There has been a terrible accident. Max was out in the street with his wheelchair. He lost control somehow, and his wheelchair went into traffic, and he was fatally injured."

A few days later, John was visiting Sheila.

"Max's last phone call was strange. He said you should read *The Tale of Two Cities*."

Sheila broke down in tears. "He knew I had read that book by Dickens. It is about a man who sacrifices himself for another man who is loved by the woman he loves. He takes the other man's place and goes to the guillotine saying, 'This is a far far better thing which I do now than I have ever done. I go to a far far better rest than I have ever known.'"

"Ah, the accident. I thought so. He felt he had to pay his dues. Another tragedy."

"God help us all, John. We all take part in the comedy and tragedy of life. The place called Golgotha is waiting for us. 'That rugged cross was my cross too.'"

This was Max's last farewell. John attended his funeral. The life insurance policy paid off, and John was able to settle the debts and started to put money away, anticipating Sheila's release.

Chapter 21

Out of Limbo Gate

John was waiting for Sheila at the prison gates. He was nervous, almost having palpitations. He was not sure what it would be like to actually be with her again, to hold her in his arms. He knew roughly when she would be released, but this was State bureaucracy, so the timing would be very variable. The gates finally opened and she walked out, the woman he had betrayed in a fit of anger but for whom he longed and for whom he had waited these two long years. His heart went bump, and he got a lump in his throat.

Sheila felt a sense of anticipation as the doors opened in front of her, then an overwhelming sense of peace. It was all behind her now—the hatred of her father, the craziness of her early promiscuous days, the disaster of Afghanistan, the drugs and alcohol, the mercy killings under Max's Svengali-like influence, the terror and the hopelessness of the trial, and the jail. She was free, and the man of her lonely hopes and dreams was waiting for her. There were times when she had hated him for his almost unforgivable lapse of trust in her and for his angry betrayal. But that was now water under the bridge. The words of her AA meetings came back to her, 'We will not forget the past, but we will close the door on it.'

She came into his arms, and they embraced for the first time in two years since she had entered jail. They brushed lips in a quick kiss as neither felt quite ready for more intimacy. Holding hands, they walked to his car.

"Not working today?"

"No. I took the day off to come here."

"You poor thing, moving to Miami and working three clinics for the last two years."

"Mostly only two, but I had to do it. Your lawyer was worth it, negotiating that plea bargain. And Max's final sacrifice paid off the rest and left enough to build a nest egg for us so that you can go and do what you want. And besides, without you, what was I going to do anyway?"

"Oh, John. It has been such a hard road."

"I am so sorry. Mea culpa."

"I have had two years with nothing to do but read. Pick your religion, I've looked at it. If you want Buddhism, it is a pretty good concept—that we are all bound on the Wheel of Life. Or we walk between the Daoist yin and yang, order and chaos. I even quite like the Norse gods—the three Fates sitting under Yggdrasil, the tree of life, spinning out our fortunes. But that is in the past. I read somewhere, and I hope that it will be true for us, 'the past with its memory of good and ill, the present with its opportunity that knows no bounds, and the future with the years that never end and know no sorrow.' John, the present is here, and the future stretches out before us. I love that line, 'I trace the rainbow through the rain, and hope the promise is not vain, that morn shall tearless be.'"

"I have been living here for two years since you were transferred to the prison in Florida. I like the medical clinics where I work. The people are good, nice guys. And my Spanish, which I learned as a resident, is now pretty good again. We can stay in Florida or move anywhere inside the US."

"No, after two years of jail here, I really don't think I want to go back to the lousy climate up north. When I was initially in jail and when we were thinking of jumping bail, I dreamed of hiding in the woods of the northwest up in the Rockies, the Cascades—you and me in a cabin in the woods in the mountains. But now I think of the isolation and the bugs. You know, I have a strange desire or dream. In jail, we look quite a lot at TV. I saw lots of ads for cruise boats leaving Port Miami. I saw condos on the edge of Biscayne Bay, just where the ships leave through the narrows. I thought that would be a fabulous place, to sit in the evening on the balcony and watch these massive cruise boats sail off and dream dreams of far-off mystical places."

"Just as long as I am with you."

"No more Tristan and Isolde. No more drama. Deus vult, just plain Sheila and John."

Later that night, they walked along Miami Beach, arm in arm. Sheila held her face up to the setting sun. John smiled down on her.

"The freedom, John, to be with you, to hold you and spend this quiet time with you, to get to know each other again and find love. Maybe we should take a cruise just to be on deck and see the ocean and feel the wind on my face, to stand at the rail with you by my side. There is a song I heard once: 'Forgotten the prison, on his windows no bars and Johnny Ramenski walked under the stars.'"

"I can take time off from the clinic, and if we go on a last-minute booking, it would be easily within our budget. I think I have enough money saved up that we can put a down payment on your condo by the water, see a decent plastic surgeon if you want for a scar revision, or sail around the world."

"Just to be with you is all I want. A cruise around the Caribbean? Maybe later. I will need to get a new passport. But first, I must look for a job. But even that can wait. I am free, free and with the man who waited for me."

"I have been reading literature and poetry to pass the time waiting for you. There is this one of Kipling's which describes us.

> Side beside because our fate
> Damned us ere our birth.
> We stole out of limbo gate
> Looking for the earth.
> Hand in pulling hand amid
> Fears, no dreams have known"

"Yes, I know that poem too. 'Sheila ran with me she did, Sheila all alone.' Max recited it to me when he suggested I look for you. But unlike that poem, we should remain together. Was it Browning? 'Oh thou Soul of my Soul, to be with you again, and may God take the rest.' Or there is this one.

> How far is St Helena to the Gate of Heavens Grace?
> That no one knows, and no one ever will.
> But fold your hands across your heart and cover up your face,
> After all you traipsing's, child, lie still!"

"I don't know that one. St. Helena? Napoleon?"
"Yes, surprisingly beautiful about such a man.

> How far is St Helena from a fight in Paris streets?
> I haven't time to answer now- the men are falling fast.
> The guns begin to thunder and the drums begin to beat.
> If you take the first step you will take the last."

"The drums and the thunder, yes, we certainly had that in Afghanistan. Would you like to visit a church to celebrate your freedom?"

"That's a thought, but I am really now a David Hume guy. If God exists, don't go bothering him. He has other things to do, other fish to fry."

"Well, yes, I think so too. Maybe we should go and eat. Morton's or Emeralds are just over there. Their cuisine is always first-class. Steak or Cajun?"

"Anywhere with you is OK. God, I feel great. Was it Adam Smith who talked about 'coming at last to that quiet harbor after the turbulent sea of life'?"

"Yes, *The Wealth of Nations* guy, but just as long as it is not his particular 'quiet harbor.' At least not yet. We have some living to do."

Chapter 22

Nero's Fiddle

Sitting peacefully on their condo balcony watching the ships enter and leave Port Miami far below them, Sheila was quietly happy. She felt comfortable enough to inquire as to someone else's motives, which she had never really done before. When she had been with John in Afghanistan, they had lived for the moment and talked of a mythical future. There had been no interest in the past.

"I never asked you, what was it you wanted from life, John?"

He was slow to answer. "I never really knew because I never really thought about it. Curious, is it not? I went through high school, six years of medical school, and six years of surgical training and no one really asked me to ask myself what I wanted from life. I am not even terribly sure why I picked medical school. It just seemed like a safe job. Once I was on the educational staircase, it was just a case of putting one foot in front of the other."

"No rebellion? No dreams?"

"Rebellion? No. There was nothing in my life to rebel against. Maybe the fact that WW1 and WW11and then socialist ideology had ruined my country. But war was a fact of life, and what to do about the ideology I loathed? It wasn't even as if I was a Royalist. Bonnie Prince Charlie, all that moron ever did for Scotland was get good men killed. I was always Cromwell's man. I remember one teacher in my high school saying things that even as a child I knew were not true, were frank nonsense and lies. God, I loathed that woman.

"But even that was not rebellion. After all, we all grew up knowing in the back of our minds that for a very long time, young, ambitious Scotsmen left Scotland. It was too small, too poor, and stuck in the middle of the North Sea. The Romans called it Ultima Thule, the end of the earth. Hadrian built a wall to keep us out of the empire. Dr. Johnson said that the best thing a young Scotsman could see was the high road to England."

"Did you resent that?"

"No. It was what it was. Neither good nor bad, like the rain, it just was. Emigration was sort of expected. No one thought it unusual. It never occurred to me to rail against anything."

"How about dreams? Did you have those?"

"Again, it is hard to remember. I guess, but what? I loved poetry but knew I had absolutely no talent to write it. I never wanted to be a painter or a physicist. A warrior, maybe. We had all sorts of stories of Scottish mercenaries and not all had wonderful endings. 'Poor Gavin, good Gavin. He came home no way at all to his mother and his mountains.' What was that poem?

> And every lad in his heart was dreaming
> of honor and wealth to come,
> And honor and noble pride were calling
> To the tune of the pipes and drum."

"I assume all kids did. Guys in my little town had fought in wars. I grew up with the tales of Napier, Colin Campbell on the Heights of Alma, and John Nicholson."

"I never heard of any of these people."

"I am not surprised. They were all generals and administrators of a bygone era. Currently, if anyone had ever heard of them, they would be looked upon as monsters of the patriarchy. John Nicholson was always the romantic one. If he had lived, he would have been the viceroy of India. Instead he ended up in a ditch with a bullet in his belly."

"What happened?"

"He was up north in India fighting in one of these everlasting Sikh Wars. The East India Company native troops rebelled, the Indian Mutiny. A bunch of useless administrators and company generals were sitting outside the walls of Delhi trying to decide what to do. When he heard of the rebellion, Nicholson marched south, deposed the East India Company commanders the evening he arrived, took charge, and stormed Delhi the next day; and the mutiny was effectively over. He led and died in the assault.

> Nicholson is dead. He died before Delhi.
> Guns of the north sing vengeance for Nicholson."

"You really wanted that?"

"No. By the time I was no longer a little boy that was not an option. Europe was in retreat everywhere. The British had left India, the Dutch, Indonesia, and the French, Vietnam. Portugal was leaving Angola and all the rest of Africa. One of the great laments played on the bagpipes was "The Barren Rocks *of* Aden," which had been a huge British military base. And they lost that too. Those fools in London could not even keep the Suez Canal, although that was probably the fault of those in the US Department of State of very, very uncertain loyalty. Foggy Bottom was full of Soviet agents. Not that it matters. It is water under the bridge."

"Yes, I suppose in the same way silly Jimmy Carter gave away the Panama Canal. Why did you go to the US?"

"Britain seemed to have lost its way. To a young Scotsman, America was still the new world. The American Dream seemed real, a place where fame and fortune awaited, where a man could still dream dreams."

"So you did your surgical training here."

"I did. But surgery became pretty boring after the first few years, so I thought I had made a mistake. Taking out gallbladders for the rest of my life did not seem very interesting. I was in practice for a few years and making good money, but then I got tired of it. When my wife left to go back to Britain, I looked around for something else to do. The movie M*A*S*H made war look like fun and excitement."

"So you enlisted. And was it what you expected it to be?"

"Like everything else in my life, I didn't know what to expect. Dashing cavalry charges, *Beau Geste*, becoming a famous military doc like Ambroise Paré or Trueta. It was none of these things. But I got by with booze and poetry."

"And then me."

"And then you. You were the bright star in my sky. I should have sent you back because of your obvious PTSD. But I wanted to keep you. I am so sorry."

"Don't be. It was not your fault. I wanted to stay. I felt I could cope."
"And then disaster."
"And then disaster. But that is over—a new chapter, a new day. The AA promises. 'We will not wish to forget the past, but we will close the door on it.' What of the future?"
"Just the quiet life with you. No real bucket list of things to do or places to go. I like the days in the clinic, being with people, helping when I can and the restful evenings with books, occasional movies, and walks on the beach. 'The long day wanes, the slow moon climbs.' And God help me, just a little tenderness. I don't ask much or expect much. I certainly did not get any the last few years of my previous marriage. So that and with you beside me, to lose myself in a little in poetry and some easy dreams is all I want.

> The long day wanes, the slow moon climbs
> The deep moans round with many voices."

"Yes. I, too, have no desire to seek a new world. This one is fine for me. But what is happening in these university campuses in the US? Look at all these riots, like the one we saw on TV last night in California over someone who was going to speak on something. What is that all about?"
"I don't know. Maybe it is just as Dostoevsky said 'that if humans were given everything so that they could fill their time with eating cake and carrying out the procreation of the species, then they would take a hammer and break it just for some excitement.'"
"Didn't Menken say something similar 'about jolly men strolling down the road heaving dead cats in sanctuaries'?"
"Yes, but these students don't seem very jolly."
"They always seem to be complaining about needing safe spaces and being oppressed and threatened by something or other."
"I know. The most privileged generation ever—no real wars, no famines, no plagues. The four horsemen of the Apocalypse have their beasts stabled. Hard to believe. I think that the root cause of the current turmoil was the introduction of the birth control pill. For the first time, sex had no consequences or almost no consequences."
"Tell me about it. I was one of those."
"You were a bit later. Woodstock, with free love and all, was the late sixties. The young guys must have been mad for it, freely available for the first time in history. Young guys would do anything for free sex, agree to

any crazy belief, go and waste four years of their lives at useless universities taking Mickey Mouse courses and learning the rubbish from the Frankfurt School and then the teachings of these evil poseurs, the postmodernists."

"Yes, that would make sense. I think it was one of the Jesuits or maybe it was Loyola himself who said that if he was given a young mind, he could control it forever."

"Was that Loyola or Cardinal Richelieu? Whoever, I think that they were correct. The students who did not believe the rubbish they were being taught eventually had enough free sex, left university, got a job, and carried on with life. Those who did believe stayed at university for free or slightly coerced love from their students and essentially no work, as none of this postmodernist crap takes any intellectual thought, and became the professors, and so the cycle closed itself. As these professors got older and got control of the hiring committees, they hired those who believed the same things and thought the same way. So now all you have in humanities at universities are these moronic or cynical beta males, angry because they think they are not being paid what they feel they are worth, Lenin's useful idiots who preach his doctrine endlessly."

"So what happens now?"

"Rome falls, and these pampered clowns die. Or they have one more attempt at socialism and then they die in the gulags. Listen on YouTube to that Russian defector Besmenov if you really want to know what will happen to them. He laid it out in the eighties what would happen, and so far, everything he said then has absolutely come true in spite of the fall of the Soviet Union."

"I have heard him. Depressing. And the rest of us?"

"God knows! Mao killed most the docs in China, and medicine in Russia was pretty awful. And yet where to escape? You remember these people who ran away to live in the Falkland Islands to escape the threat of nuclear war. And then the Argies invaded, and then the British army threw them out. So rather than escape, they experienced war up close and personal. I don't know where we could be safe. Maybe Japan, but they don't want immigrants."

"Ah Jesus, John. You are as cheerful as Max, and your vision of the future is just as bleak. Maybe the serenity prayer will see us through."

She reached out and, holding hands, together they said the prayer, "God, grant me the serenity to accept the things I cannot change, the courage to change the things I can, and the wisdom to know the difference."

Chapter 23

Turmoil in the Old World

Sheila found work at one of the walk-in clinics that was employing John as a nonoperating surgeon. She had lost her nurse's license after her conviction, so she found work as a receptionist. With her nursing training, she soon became a valued member of the front desk team at the clinic. After the teething problems natural with any new job, they settled into a quiet life with regular hours. If there was any need for extra money, John would simply do a few more shifts at either of the clinics he worked.

One evening, after a simple supper, sitting on their condo balcony reading, quietly happy with each other's company, Sheila lifted her head and looked for a long time at a gigantic cruise boat leaving PortMiami. John saw where she was looking.

"Sheila, we can afford it financially. Would you like to take a cruise?"

"Sure, but where? The Caribbean, the Far East, or Europe? I am from Toronto, and I have no desire to see Alaska. I saw enough snow as a child. I don't want to see it again."

"I don't know where. I have never been on a cruise before. Maybe just around the Caribbean to see if we like it."

"Why not? Sounds fine to me. Let me look at the internet and maybe get some brochures. Maybe go some off-peak time this winter as that will be a lot cheaper. If we like it, maybe the Mediterranean next summer."

They found a reasonably priced cruise in one of the better cruise lines and loved it. The long lazy days were refreshing. They would get up before dawn and walk on the promenade deck, sipping a cappuccino from the early coffee counter, watching the sun come up and often the boat dock at that day's destination. There would then be a leisurely breakfast. They took a couple of excursions at the ports the ship docked but found them not much fun. There was very little that was visually different on the islands, and in Florida, they virtually lived on the beach anyway.

They got into the habit of going to the gym, which, by that time of day, was usually more or less empty, and would work out for an hour or two. They would then disembark and walk around the port they were in. There was nothing particularly different to buy that they could not buy in Miami and nothing they really wanted anyway. Then a long lazy lunch followed by a little table tennis or some other activity or an hour or two during the heat of the day reading in the ship's well-stocked library and then a little afternoon tea. Never having that before, they found it an absolutely delightful custom with its varieties of teas, tiny sandwiches, and pastries while listening to some stringed-instrument chamber music. There would then be another long, long walk on the deck, watching the boat leave the dock and the sun begin to set.

After a leisurely dinner, they went to see the show provided by the cruise boat a couple of times. As expected, the show was a little tedious, but they appreciated the performer's efforts. They preferred to be on deck, talking quietly, listening to the ocean slide by, and looking at the vault of heaven with the moon and the stars. John quoted the poem to Sheila.

> Cross that rules the Southern sky
> Stars that sweep and turn and fly
> Sing the Lover's Litany
> Love like ours can never die.

They embraced, and leaning on the rails, Sheila quoted her own poem to him.

> We have had enough of action and of motion we,
> Rolled to larboard, rolled to starboard
> When the surge was seething free,
> Where the wallowing monster spouted
> His foam fountains on the sea.

"I am not sure we want to become lotus eaters, but it has certainly been turbulent," said John. "The present quiet harbor is so good I am afraid it may not last."

Living as they did in Florida, there was no desire to sit around the inevitably crowded onboard pool. The other thing they found, which they had heard of and hoped existed, was that most afternoons, at about cocktail hour, there was a Friends of Bill meeting for those with alcohol problems. They were surprised to see how well-attended these meetings were. They were all too aware that so-called controlled drinking was a myth; all it would take would be one shot of alcohol and the desire circuits in the brain would open and they would be back on that wide-open slippery road to hell. They knew that alcohol remained for both of them 'cunning, baffling and powerful.'

"Funny how much I managed to screw up my life because I worried about what my family thought of me," said Sheila, "but then I found you and no longer care."

"All I wanted was a little love, a little appreciation of my efforts, not too much to ask, one might have thought, but actually very difficult to get. Patients gave it to me in spades but not so much in my personal life. Maybe because the patients gave it to me without asking I never learned how to ask, and so they spoiled me for the real world. I wonder if all docs have the same problem. Looking back, I wonder if that was not my problem. Maybe I did not have the patience and the humanity to listen to my poor wife in her moments of doubt and terror. I always thought that it was her fault I got on the booze and that I was being the noble one for staying around. Maybe it was me who was the problem. Maybe if I had been kinder and more understanding, it would have been better."

"The past is past, John. All our yesterdays,

> The Moving Finger writes; and having writ
> Moves on: not all thy Piety nor Wit
> Shall lure it back to cancel half a Line,
> Not all thy Tears wash out a Word of it.
> Ah love could thou and I with fate conspire
> To grasp this sorry scheme of things entire,
> Would we not shatter it to bits?
> And then remold it nearer heart's desire."

"*The Rubáiyát*, yes. 'Ah Moon of my Delight that knows no wane.' Never leave me, Sheila."

"I never will."

Living so close to PortMiami, they escaped the unavoidable hassle that most passengers have at debarkation at the end of the cruise, rushing to make plane connections to take them back where they had come from. The pair simply walked around the deck waiting for the crowds to clear before they left. They enjoyed their Caribbean cruise so much that they made arrangements to cruise around Europe that summer with the same cruise line.

They flew into Athens where neither had been previously. They intended to stay and explore for a couple of days before boarding the ship at Piraeus, the port of Athens. Like all tourists, they climbed the acropolis to see the Parthenon and wandered around the ruins of a fallen civilization who had built these still-magnificent structures.

"So this is where it all began?" said Sheila.

"Yes, the cradle of Western civilization."

"And this is all that is left?"

"Yes. The Turks who had conquered Greece used the temple to store gunpowder, and of course, it blew up during one of their wars."

"It must have been quite something before that happened. Why did they do that?"

"I guess for the same reason the Taliban in Afghanistan blew up these centuries-old famous statues of Buddha, and ISIS did its best to destroy everything they could in the territories they conquered, especially Palmyra the magnificent. For them, the past never existed, and I guess they are trying to make sure it never existed for anyone else either, including the people like these poor Christian Yezidis in the Middle East on whom they are committing genocide as fast as they can. God help these poor Christians because no one else is lifting a finger to do so."

"Lordy, Lordy. How awful. That useless Pontiff. Max called him the Antichrist. He sits in Rome and says nothing about the genocide of the Christians. But let's not talk about that anymore. There is nothing we can do. Let's have some lunch."

They walked down from the Parthenon, had some lunch on a patio from which they could see the Acropolis, and then decided to walk through thePlaka, now a tourist area of little alleyways and narrow roads full of bars and cafes and little shops packed with antiques and standard tourist kitsch. John remembered having been told by his friends when he was a student in Scotland that this was a place famous for drinking, dancing, fun, and games. It was quite crowded. John suddenly felt something touch him and grabbed at his pants pocket where he kept his wallet. He felt a hand in his pocket. He tried to hold it, but the owner pulled his hand out and ran off. John made to follow him, but then realized that his wallet was still there. He had no wish to follow the thief up a narrow, twisting alleyway. He had no idea what might be waiting as the place seemed full of young men just standing around. He breathed a sigh of relief that his wallet was still there, that he had escaped the incredible hassle of trying to replace passport, money, and credit cards in a foreign country.

That episode left them very wary and distrustful. From then on, when they were in any place with crowds, he kept his hand firmly on his wallet. The next day they did take a tourist coach trip down to the Peloponnese and, shepherded around by the tour guide, saw the ancient theatre at Epidaurus and marveled at its incredible acoustics and had lunch on a balcony at Nafplio overlooking the Mediterranean.

Gusts of wind blowing in over the water did indeed make it look like Homer's 'wine dark sea' and reduced a little the bad taste left by the pickpocket. They both promised that someday they would read the Odyssey. Not wanting to spend any more time in Athens, the next morning, they got a taxi to the docks and boarded the cruise boat as soon as they could. The moment of fear when John thought he had lost his wallet to the pickpocket removed any desire to revisit Greece.

They found the cruise boat delightful. As before, they would get up before dawn, get a coffee, walk on the deck, and watch the sun come up and the boat dock in a new port. They took a couple of excursions; but even having no high expectations, they found them long, crowded, and tedious. They simply got into the habit of walking around the local town close to the dock rather than spend hours on a tourist bus. It was the sailing itself that they preferred, looking at the ocean glide by as they strolled the promenade deck arm in arm with the wind on their face. In the evenings, they preferred to rent a movie or pick up a book from the ship's library.

The day before the boat was due to stop in Sicily, they looked at the tour options, including an excursion to the still-active volcano Etna or the attraction of the clifftop city of Taormina, which had been a tourist destination for more than one thousand years.

"The crowds will be such that it is not likely to be worth the effort," said Sheila.

John agreed but did wonder about going to Syracuse.

"Why there?" asked Sheila.

"When I was a student, I knew a girl from there who told me about it. It has one of the horrors of the ancient world. Six thousand Athenians were taken prisoner by the king of Syracuse when they lost a battle and were sent down into his underground quarry. They never saw the light of day again. The quarry is still there."

"Oh od. I don't want to see that. We have already seen enough horrors in Afghanistan to do for the rest of our lives, and look at the hours on the bus to get there."

"You are right. It is too depressing and not worth it. I know the history of the disaster of Alcibiades, so I don't need to see the actual site."

"Wasn't Syracuse where Archimedes was killed?"

"Yes, but that was another battle, against Rome. Let's just go for a walk around Catania. That is an ancient city in its own right."

"OK, sure, let's do that. Have breakfast, go to the gym, and get off the boat after all the tour buses have left."

They followed that plan and strolled out of the guarded dock gates into the town. The main square, the Piazza del Duomo, was only a short walk away and, as always in these ancient cities, was spectacular in the way that modern cities never are.

"It is almost as if modern town planners and architects have forgotten how to design anything," said Sheila.

"Yes, think of the communist brutalist school. I was in Dresden once. The professor there told me that the destruction done by the communist architects and builders was worse than that done by the allied bombers. They produced the most horrible buildings in the whole world. Not only was the design terrible, the materials were worse, and the buildings were already falling down. I think the decline of architecture began after WWI with the French like Le Corbusier. They built purely utilitarian buildings with no beauty and no eye to the future. In a decade or two, all these glass boxes will be pulled down and replaced by new glass boxes. Whereas a piazza like this will continue to exist and be used for the rest of time. The buildings here are more than a thousand years old and still look gorgeous while the center of Detroit is a vision of a dystopian hell. The modern planners seem to despise the people they are supposed to serve." John stopped. "Sorry, Sheila. I am sorry. Another rant. I am turning into just another bitter old man lost in the glories of the past."

"Yes, but it is hard not to be when one has seen the awful downtown Detroit. But that looks like an open-air tourist mall over in the corner. Probably it is full of the usual tourist kitsch, but at least it is colorful, and maybe we can stop and get a cup of coffee."

They strolled down the mall, obviously a street converted into something for tourists. There were people but far fewer than they had anticipated in a major destination for cruise lines bringing people to see the world-famous city of Taormina. They saw nothing in the shops in which they were remotely interested, so they strolled further into the town. It appeared increasingly dilapidated, so with little else to see, they felt that they might as well head back to the boat. The town seemed to be laid out in a grid pattern, so they decided to head directly back to the dock. Some of the streets were narrow and a little dark, but they thought nothing of that.

Sheila noted that the streets and alleys seemed to have a lot of young men hanging about doing nothing. By now, it was 11:00 a.m., so they assumed that everyone who had a job would be at work. The young men did not look Italian but looked more North African or like the people they knew from Afghanistan. Becoming a little nervous at the brazen stares of the young men, they quickened their pace as they knew the docks could only be two or three blocks away. Halfway down the street they were on, they noticed four young men standing at the door of a small cafe. They openly stared at the couple as they approached. Another two young men came out of the cafe to join them. Sheila looked back. It was a short street, and they were almost equidistant from either end. She thought of retreating but then thought, *This is Italy, not Afghanistan or some of the worst of the US inner cities. This is a major tourist destination. It must be safe here. They would surely have told us if it was not.*

No sooner had she had that thought and reached for John's arm when the young men surrounded the couple. One reached out and squeezed her breasts. John tried to push him away, but another grabbed him from behind; and while he was held, another punched him so hard in the stomach that if he had not been held, he would have fallen down. The others attacked her in earnest, ripping open her blouse and bra and reaching between her legs. She screamed as loudly as she could but thought in despair, *In Italy in the middle of the day. In a tourist zone.*

She was so distracted trying to fend them off that she barely heard running footsteps behind her. She thought, *More of them are coming to join in. This is the mass rape of Colonge or Tahrir Square all over again.* Suddenly a rifle butt-crashed into the face of one of her attackers, knocking him down. A second was also hit, and the crowd backed off, unhanding her and John. Their rescuers were two young Italian soldiers who stood guns at the ready. The attackers stood their ground defiantly, helping up those who had been knocked down, daring the soldiers to open fire. They seemed completely unafraid of the guns in the soldier's hands. Sheila thought nervously, *they probably know that the guns will never be fired, and given the state of European security, they may not even be loaded.* It looked like a classic Mexican standoff.

Two of her attackers were standing menacingly and provocatively close. One of the soldiers, a big young bull of a man, suddenly pivoted, graceful as a ballerina, and doing what Sheila later learned was called a side snap kick, drove his full weight against the extended knee of the attacker standing closest. Sheila watched with satisfaction as the knee bent back into an impossible angle. *There goes his knee ligaments,* she thought. *Limp on that for the rest of your life, you bastard.*

Amazingly, the young soldier continued the pivot and, with the same foot, kicked the next man on the side of the face, knocking him down. Seeing the two boldest of the would-be rapists down on the ground, the rest turned tail and ran. The young soldier kicked the knee man in the ribs so hard he lifted him off the ground, causing the rapist to scream, and then kicked him in the face. The other young soldier stamped hard with his booted foot a couple of times on the outstretched hand of the other man lying on the ground. Sheila and John backed off. The more aggressive soldier, obviously recognizing that they were tourists, turned to them, speaking English.

"It will be OK now. These people will not come back for a while. You are from a cruise boat, no?"

"Yes," said John, "and we would like to go back there. We cannot thank you enough." And he pulled out his wallet.

"No, no," said the soldier, "we are just doing our job. Or rather, we are doing the job the police should be doing but are not. These people are not Italian. I am deeply embarrassed. I do not understand what these EU bureaucrats and that Merkel are doing bringing these people here. They are flooding into Europe, and the crime rate is astronomical. Let us escort you back to your ship."

"Are you going to call the police?"

"Why bother? The police won't do anything because even if they arrest them, the jails are full of migrants, so the judges won't convict. Or if they do they are let out immediately.

"That was quite a demonstration," said John admiringly.

"You mean the kicks? That is Brazilian fighting. I am a member of a club. This is the first time I have actually been able to use it in real life."

"Does this sort of thing happen often?" asked John.

"It is not as bad as Germany or Sweden, where it is getting very unsafe for a woman to walk alone, but it is getting bad, even here in the South. Women have to be careful. My cousin lives in Milan, and he says it is bad up there. None of us understand this. There is a 40 percent youth unemployment for young Italians in the South, and we are bringing in more people. To do what other than sit on welfare? This is a disaster. As soon as my military service is up, I want to go to America. The Risorgimento, the reunification of Italy, was a disaster for the South from which we have never recovered, and joining the EU made it even worse. There is no hope and no future here."

"We have our own problems, but yes, it is better than here." He gave the soldier his name card. "If you need help with sponsorship, just call me."

"*Graze*. You may be hearing from me very soon," said the soldier. "But here is the gate into the dock. It is guarded so you will be safe inside. If you are stopping any other places in Europe, remember that they are all the same. Go with a tour group and do not wander off on your own. You may wander into an area where Europeans are not allowed."

"Not allowed?" asked Sheila, holding her torn clothes closed as best she could.

"We call them no-go zones. They are only for migrants, no one else—not the police, not the garbage collectors, not even the fire service often."

"I heard it was bad," said John. "But I had no idea."

"Yes. They steal the equipment off the fire trucks. I doubt that Merkel or any of these clowns in Brussels have any idea either, or if they have, they completely ignore it. Anyway, we must be on our way. You were fortunate that we were on our way home. Arrivederci. Be safe!" The two soldiers waved goodbye and turned away.

"After this, I am not getting off the boat," said Sheila.

"Absolutely, Europe can keep its cities and cathedrals. I am so sorry you were attacked, Sheila. I had no idea that things were as bad. Obviously the media hides just how bad it is. They barely mention it."

"I will never leave America again, maybe not even on a cruise boat. Or if we are on a cruise boat, I am not sure I want to get off it. God, I hope the US does not go the same way. These people have recreated Kandahar in Europe."

"How sad. How infinitely sad," said John. "The end of civilization as we have known it. The Enlightenment is over. I guess it is to conceal just how bad it is that they put that comedian in Scotland in jail for telling a joke."

"A comedian in jail? For a joke about what?"

"I am not sure. But from the state of this town and the media silence, it was probably a joke about migrants. That is the only way they could keep a mess like this a secret."

"God help us all. What is the world coming to? I need a drink."

"No, Sheila. Don't even joke about that. 'Anyone can fight the battle for one day.' Let's go on board and have some lunch. There is no need for us to get off the boat again until we disembark in Monte Carlo to get a flight back to the US. Rome and Florence we can look at on YouTube. There is no need for us to physically go there. It looks like Rome has fallen to the barbarians again. The Dark Ages are coming back to Europe."

"How sad. How terribly sad."

Chapter 24

High Noon

"I think we are low on soft drinks, so I'll just drop into the drug store here and get some to take home."

"Fine, John. I'll drop into this store for a minute. They seem to have some new fall fashions."

Sheila went into the clothing store and looked around. Most of the clothing were standard cheap Florida goods, but at the back, there seemed to be something interesting. They had just finished their shifts at the clinic where they both worked and were strolling to the car park at the end of the street intending to drive home. They had no particular plans for that evening—maybe a stroll on the beach or maybe a quiet early supper on the balcony of their condo overlooking the exit to PortMiami, looking at the cruise boats sailing off.

After a few minutes, Sheila wondered what was taking John so long. The drug store had not looked that busy. She heard a volley of pops. She was confused, then suddenly it registered. She had heard these unmistakable noises before, many times before, in that god-awful place of her downfall, Afghanistan. She never expected to hear gunfire in the streets of Miami. She ran out of the store. Across the street she could see the open door of the drug store. There was a man lying face down, partially out of the store, his body wedging the door open. He lay with the stillness of the dead. There were more shots from inside the store. A heavily bearded man appeared at the door, brandishing a pistol. He shot at three passersby who had stopped to stare at the commotion, obviously unaware that these had been gunshots. One fell and the other two began to run, one with a grotesque limp. The pedestrians on the street scattered. The bearded man disappeared inside the store.

Sheila noted with a gasp of relief that the dead man wedged in the door was not John. She knew immediately what was happening. Such affairs were now common in Europe, and she had heard of it occurring also in Australia. It was a terrorist hostage-taking. There would be the inevitable impossible demands, and then one by one the hostages would be killed. She and John had discussed the likelihood that this would soon begin to happen in the US, but for some reason, she had not expected it in Miami. And yet here it was; she was face-to-face with the nightmare.

She had no idea what to do. John carried a gun as he had a concealed weapons permit. Maybe he would get a chance to use it. It would depend on how many hostage takers there were. If it was a lone wolf, John would likely kill the terrorist. The fact that he had not already done so suggested that more than one terrorist was hiding behind the hostages. *Three, almost certainly three of them,* she thought.

She herself did not carry a gun, but she had practiced with John at the gun range because they both were aware of the violence on the street, and having been in Afghanistan, both took personal security seriously. There was a spare gun registered in John's name in the glove compartment of their car, which was parked in the lot at the end of the street. Sheila took off running.

Opening the car door, she took the gun, a flat 9mm automatic, from the glove compartment and, to conceal it, pushed it into the rear waistband of her skirt under her jacket and hurried back. Already there were police at the scene. One had incautiously approached the store and had been shot himself and was lying face down on the street in front of the store.

The bearded man again appeared at the door and shouted that if anyone approached, the hostages would be killed. One small child was dragged into the open door, shot in the head, and tossed into the empty street. Sheila, hiding behind a parked car, groaned in despair.

The street was silent. With wailing sirens, more police arrived and began to surround the store, stringing yellow tape. The crowds had melted away. Within minutes, a negotiator arrived with a bullhorn. The same bearded man appeared at the door, shouting something incomprehensible. Another child was dragged into view. Inside the store, there was a volley of shots and screams, then silence. The child was dragged into view again, shot in the head, and thrown onto the sidewalk.

Sheila knew what had happened. She could visualize the scene. Someone had tried to run when the shooters first showed their guns. He had been shot down at the door. The shoppers, staff, and children would be wedged into a corner with almost certainly two gunmen menacing them. There would have to be two to leave the spokesman at the door. One child had been executed and thrown onto the street. That was so barbaric and unexpected that no one would have had any time to react. When they took the second child, John and whatever men were prisoners inside the store would have reacted. John was Scots American. Very few men with a heritage like that could sit through the cold-blooded execution of a child.

Feminists had tried to chase the manhood out of the men of the West and largely had succeeded with the rise of soy boys and beta males. But there was still a vestige of cold-blooded courage left, men who could make themselves do what they felt they had to do regardless of the consequences. That residual belief was still present in a few of the men of John's generation. These men would not, could not, look on the execution of children and do nothing. He would have pulled out his gun and started firing. Hopefully, he would have killed one terrorist before the others shot him down. He would be in there, lying on the floor in front of the children he had tried to protect, bleeding and dying or most likely dead.

Sheila knew that as clearly as she knew anything. She felt the lump in her throat. He was dead. These bastards had killed the only one who had ever mattered in her whole rotten, miserable life. And what would happen to them? They would be jailed, and then some piece of garbage in Congress would be asking for a pardon for them as poor, misunderstood freedom fighters. These murderers would be treated like political prisoners and released after a few years. The Miami SWAT team would kill them if given a chance, but if the standoff continued for long enough, these useless clowns, these deep state FBI eunuchs would take over and eventually let them go free. "Well, fuck that."

She rose to her feet and ducked under the police tape, evading the attempts of the police to restrain her. Across the street, she stopped running and slowed to a walk. Holding her hands out from her sides, she approached the open door. She forced a wide smile on her face.

High noon, she thought. *Gary Cooper. No, Clint Eastwood. Make my day!*

The bearded one appeared at the door, pointing his pistol at her. She smiled more widely at him, and he stepped back inside. The street was silent. As she stepped over the dead man at the door and entered, she saw

John on the floor and felt the dopamine blast hit her. Time slowed down as her visual frames' per-second processing jumped sky-high. The inside of the store got brighter, and everything sharpened into focus. She could see the second man on her left out of the corner of her eye holding a gun on her. John was lying on his side in front of the hostages, who were crammed into the corner as she had known they would be. One terrorist was sitting against the wall with his knees up, holding his belly with both hands. She knew John had shot that one.

She reached behind, felt the gun butt, and pulled it out. The first man was in front of her. His eyes widened as he saw the gun, but she gut shot him before he could do anything. There was an explosion of pain in her left shoulder, and she was spun to the left. She knew she had been shot. She brought up her gun. She saw the gun that had shot her coming down. Her own gun came up, and they both fired. She felt another hammer blow in her gut and went down, still holding her gun. She saw the second man she had shot fall.

The rage and fear for John was hot in her, giving her power as she struggled up on her knees. The one who had shot her was facedown. The first man was on his side not far from her. He looked at her. She put the muzzle of the gun almost in his eye and shot him. Overcome with weakness, she almost went down again; but by sheer willpower, she forced herself up to look at the man sitting against the wall. He saw her gun coming up and lifted both bloodstained hands from his belly in supplication. "Please," he said pleadingly.

The rage burned in her. "Fuck you, asshole," she said, taking careful aim and grinned as his nose disappeared. "Good shot," she said to herself.

Again, the weakness overcame her, and she went face down on the floor, her left arm out, the gun still clutched in her right hand. The stunned hostages jumped to their feet and began to run for the door. The first was a heavy young man. In his haste, he stepped on her left hand but kept running. The pain in her hand brought her up.

"You fucking soy boy. You cowardly son of a bitch. You did nothing to help John."

Had she had the strength she would have shot him in the back, but he was out of the door before she could raise her gun. They all ran, all of the hostages, women dragging their children. Left in the silent store, there were only the three dead terrorists, herself, and John lying there. She got to her hands and knees and crawled to him. With the last of her strength, she turned him. She sat cross-legged, his head on her lap. His eyes blinked open, and he looked up at her. "I waited for you," he said clearly. His eyes closed, and his breathing stopped. She knew he was dead.

"Oh Jesus Christ," she said. "John. No. No." She held his head in her hands and bent over and kissed his forehead. "Oh my love."

All she could see before her was a waste of empty days, loneliness, and despair—no love, no one to share her little dreams, her hopes, the small joys of day to day, nothing. The man she loved was gone, her only love. She could not face the world without him. *Maybe, maybe he will be waiting for me on the other side of the river.*

She still had the gun in her right hand. She put the barrel in her mouth and pulled the trigger.

Chapter 25

Requiem

The SWAT team leader, having sidled along the wall of the building, was about to cautiously peer in a window as he had heard nothing since the hostages escaped. He pulled back at the gunshot. That was followed by profound silence, so he cautiously raised his head again. He could see nothing moving, so he gestured to his men, and they came barreling in through the door, guns at the ready. He saw two dead terrorists scattered around the door and one slumped against the wall. A man lay on the floor with his head on a woman's lap. She was folded over him. The back of her head was blown off.

He had watched this woman run under the police tape, cross the street, and walk into the open door. There had been numerous shots, and then the flood of hostages came running out. He was appalled. This woman had saved everyone, and then clearly taken her own life. He had been a SWAT team leader for a long time and thought that he had seen everything, but this was different.

Tears came into his eyes. "God rest her brave soul," he said gruffly, turning away.

The media, as usual, barely reported the event. Friends in their AA group took care of the funeral as no one knew of any relatives. A friend, at the close of the simple oration, quoted a hymn they had both liked.

> Oh love that seekest me through pain
> I cannot close my heart to thee.

I trace the rainbow through the rain
And feel the promise is not vain
That morn shall tearless be.

Oh cross that liftest up my head
I dare not ask to fly from thee.
I lay in dust life's glory dead
But from the ground there blossoms red
Life that shall endless be.

Envoi

One of the problems of life is the ending of it. Few people look on death as 'that quiet harbor after the turbulent sea of life.' The collapse of birth rates, among other factors, has led to the demise of the three-generation family in the West. Retirement homes struggle to deal with the flood of increasingly infirm, occasionally confused, and sometimes violent elderly. Western legal systems equally have no idea of how to cope with this modern dilemma.

The main protagonist, Sheila, an unwanted child, in retaliation, throws herself into a destructive life. Eventually realizing the futility of that, she becomes a military nurse. Shipped to Afghanistan, she finds love amid the horror and maelstrom of war. A tragic episode finds her dismissed from the military suffering from PTSD and addictions. Painfully overcoming that, she finds work in a retirement home where she falls under the sway of a Svengali-like figure who discusses at length with her the end-of-life dilemma and encourages her to undertake some mercy killings, initially to protect him.

She reunites with her surgeon lover from Afghanistan, who has his own problems. A tragic misunderstanding results in her being charged for the mercy killings and jailed. On her release, she and her lover enjoy peace for a time before being involved in a final violent confrontation with evil.

The main characters share a love of poetry and literature. As one says, 'everything that should be said has already been said by someone else, only better.' In consequence, this story contains numerous quotations on the issues of love, life, and death.

About the Authors

Hugh Cameron is an orthopedic surgeon, originally from Scotland, who lives and works in Toronto. He was one of the original developers of modern artificial joints, especially the almost universally used technology of anchoring the implants to the bone. For more than thirty years, he crisscrossed the world teaching these surgical skills. He has published several books—two being technical on surgery, one autobiographical, and several fiction.

Edna Quammie is an operating room nurse, originally from Connecticut. They met in Toronto General in the early seventies and have worked together off and on for almost fifty years.

They have previously coauthored a book entitled *The Big House*, which is a lighthearted description of life in the operating room in Toronto General Hospital in the seventies.

While lunching together, the question of mercy killings in nursing homes arose as a result of a discussion of a recent case widely reported in Canadian media. With almost a century of combined clinical experience, intrigued, they researched this issue. This book explores some of the dilemmas of modern medicine, especially the end-of-life care of the elderly in nursing homes, seen through the eyes of fictional characters who not only have to face this issue but who, like almost all humans, have their own issues and are grappling with some common, fairly intractable emotional problems themselves.

The years of clinical experience have impressed upon the authors the indomitable nature of many people, of how they somehow find the ability to 'trace the rainbow through the rain, and find the promise is not vain, that morn shall tearless be.'

CPSIA information can be obtained
at www.ICGtesting.com
Printed in the USA
LVHW030717130220
646756LV00001B/1